Norby and Yobo's Great Adventure

NORBY AND YOBO'S GREAT ADVENTURE

by
Janet and Isaac
Asimov

Walker and Company
New York

First published in the United States of America in 1989 by Walker Publishing Company, Inc.

Published simultaneously in Canada by Thomas Allen & Son Canada, Limited, Markham, Ontario

Library of Congress Cataloging-in-Publication Data

Asimov, Janet.
    Norby and Yobo's great adventure / by Janet and Isaac Asimov.
        p.   cm.
    Summary: When Jeff and his robot Norby accompany Admiral Yobo to prehistoric times so the admiral can do family research, the trip turns into a dangerous adventure.
    ISBN 0-8027-6893-8.—ISBN 0-8027-6894-6 (lib. bdg.)
    [1. Robots—Fiction.   2. Science fiction.   3. Space and time--Fiction.]   I. Asimov, Isaac, 1920-   .   II. Title.
PZ7.A836Nnb   1989
[Fic]—dc20   89-9146
                                                                CIP
                                                                 AC

Printed in the United States of America

10   9   8   7   6   5   4   3   2

To the cosmonauts and astronauts who keep
the dream alive.

Contents

Norby and Yobo's Great Adventure

1.

Down to Mars

Norby's dome-shaped hat popped up as if someone had pulled the knob on top. Under the wide brim Norby's front pair of eyes blinked rapidly, so the chances were good that his emotive circuits were agitated.

"What's the matter?" asked Norby's owner, Jefferson Wells. "What's so important that the admiral couldn't explain by visiphone?"

When Admiral Boris Yobo summoned Jeff and Norby to his office in the great rotating wheel of Space Command, it usually meant that they were in trouble. At the moment, Jeff was the cadet on duty for the entire long weekend, which had just begun, so Norby had gone to see Yobo alone.

It was quiet in the Space Academy library, where Jeff was studying. The old-time print book he was reading was silent, and there wasn't a peep out of the nearby bank of computer monitors, ready to warn the cadet on duty about problems anywhere in the academy.

"What have we done?" Jeff asked. It had been so wonderfully quiet—for a while.

Norby teetered back and forth on his two-way feet and said, "I have some good news and some bad news, Jeff." He flung his extendable arms out from the small metal barrel of his body. "Which do you want first?"

"The bad news. Then I can relax, knowing the worst."

"Admiral Yobo wants me to help him with his latest project."

"That sounds like the good news, especially if I don't have to help, too. I can study all weekend. . . ."

1

"I told the admiral I wouldn't do it without you."

"Norby! I'm on duty!"

"You'll be taken off duty for the purpose. And you haven't heard the good news. The admiral is very happy about this particular project."

"I'm glad he's happy, but please go without me, Norby. I don't want to be involved in another one of his projects. I still haven't recovered from the time he was recording bass renditions of ancient African chants and roped me in as baritone. I wonder if his grandnephew appreciated them."

"Jeff . . ."

"And that time he was composing epic poetry in Martian Swahili, which at least didn't give me indigestion the way his cooking craze did—all those spicy Martian recipes. I suppose I should be grateful that he no longer does the martial arts he enjoyed when he was young—"

"This project is dangerous!"

Jeff perked up. "Why didn't you say so? But how can it be dangerous if it's here in Space Command?"

"It isn't. It is also beneath my dignity."

"How can anything dangerous be beneath your dignity? And besides, the admiral has enough dignity for both of you."

"The admiral wants me to help him with his new hobby of holography. He has an expensive camera—"

"And you're afraid you'll damage it?"

"Certainly not! I'm afraid of going to his home on Mars."

"Wow! That's great! I've always wanted to see the admiral's home. It doesn't sound like a dangerous adventure but I want to go with you anyway."

Norby made a small grinding noise in his innards, and his half a head sank into his barrel so that only the tops of his eyes showed. A robot made by an Old Terran spacer from a mixture of Terran and alien machinery has unusual talents, among them the ability to look pathetic.

"It's dangerous, Jeff! I've heard that the admiral has a

2

mean, nasty older sister, and even worse, one of his grand-nephews is staying there and will want to take me apart."

Jeff laughed. "Don't be silly, Norby. The Yobos are a very distinguished Martian family, and besides, I won't let anybody touch you. I'm going to pack. I suppose I should study but it's boring here in the academy with everyone gone. Now I'm looking forward to this weekend."

"I'm not," said Norby.

Inside Yobo's private minicruiser, *The Pride of Mars*, Norby took the controls while Jeff dutifully admired the new camera equipment and wondered about the fanatical gleam in the admiral's eyes.

"Just take us halfway down to Mars," Yobo said absently, stroking the sleek cover of his camera.

"We're halfway now," Norby said. It didn't take long to go "down" because Space Command, with Space Academy attached, was in orbit around Mars.

"Good. Hold her here. I'll put on my space suit, and you come outside with me, Norby. Then you can take movies of me against the ship, with Mars beyond. Visually dramatic, I'd say. Then I'll go inside and wave from my porthole while you take more movies."

Jeff grinned. Yobo was proud of the porthole he'd had specially constructed so he could see outside without having to use the viewscreen.

In a space suit Yobo was an awesome sight. Jeff was tall for his age, but the admiral was much taller and broader. His bald head gleamed inside his transparent helmet and he hummed an old Space Command song as Norby towed him out of the ship's airlock.

While Norby's speech did not transmit through space, Jeff could hear every word relayed from the admiral's suit radio to the ship's computer. By touching the admiral Norby could communicate with him telepathically, for Yobo, like Jeff, had once been bitten by a dragon—but that's another story.*

"Make the photocomposition artistic, if you can wrap your mixed-up circuits around the concept," Yobo said, letting go of Norby and striking a heroic pose outside the ship.

Jeff thought it was amusing to watch a fat little robot wield a holocamera while hanging in space by means of minianti-grav and propulsion stabilizers (or whatever he was using to stay in one place), but when Yobo slowly turned upside down in his heroic pose, Jeff began to laugh.

"Blast it!" shouted Yobo. "Norby, you turn, too, so no one will notice that I can't control my position in space!"

Jeff couldn't stop. He laughed so hard, rocking in the control chair, that he leaned back too far and his elbow touched the control board.

The *Pride* dropped down away from Yobo and toward Mars, the scenic backdrop the admiral had wanted for the movie of his space walk. Yobo yelped and tried to propel himself toward the ship.

Jeff grappled with the controls and stopped the plunge into the thin Martian atmosphere, while Norby zoomed toward Yobo, clutched his helmet, and steered him to the airlock.

Back inside, Yobo scowled as he removed his suit. "Well, did you get the picture, Norby?"

"Yes, sir. I am efficient. Not like humans." Norby gestured in Jeff's direction.

"Ah well, no harm done," Yobo said, affable once more. "I haven't been in a space suit for years. Wonderful sensation. Have you ever tried it, Jeff?"

"Yes, sir, but it's even better without a suit, inside Norby's invisible personal field."

"Yes, I forgot you can do that." Yobo hung up his suit and marched to the control room. "Now we'll go on down to

*See *Norby's Other Secret*.

4

Mars, where my sister is working on a case in her law office this weekend, I hope. Perhaps I've mentioned her before?"

"Yes, sir."

"She's older. Much older. In fact, well into middle age, while I of course am still in my prime."

"Yes, sir."

"But it doesn't really matter if she's there," Yobo said reflectively, "since we won't be staying at my home."

"We won't?" Jeff asked, disappointed. He'd packed his weekend bag with special care in order to live up to the elegance of the Yobos.

"We'll live in the *Pride*. The only reason we're going to Mars is to pick up something from the house. And we might as well have"— Yobo looked at his watch—"tea. We should be in time for that family tradition. The butler serves it no matter who's there. If my sister's home, we probably won't be able to pack extra provisions for the ship, but I have plenty from Space Command, in addition to the latest thing in food synthesizers. We won't go hungry."

Such a thing had never crossed Jeff's mind, since he knew the admiral's fondness for good food. "If we're not staying on Mars, Admiral, where are we going?"

"That depends on Norby."

"Me, sir?"

"Yes, you. If I request it sometime, do you think you'll be able to channel your hyperdrive ability to the *Pride*'s computer?"

"Yes, sir. I can turn any ship into a hyperdrive ship as long as I stay at the controls."

Yobo nodded. "You'd better. The Federation is still trying to make another experimental hyperdrive ship to replace the one we lost through your fault."

"It wasn't my fault!" shouted Norby.

"Whatever," said Yobo. "At any rate, the Federation is still stuck here in the solar system of good old Sol, while you can go just about anywhere, can't you?"

"Certainly, sir." Norby's half a head rose to its full extent and he saluted by touching the brim of his hat.

Jeff's eyebrows raised. Norby was not ordinarily given to displays of correct military subservience. Perhaps he was trying to persuade himself that Yobo had an important mission in mind for him.

"Ah," Yobo said with a deep breath that expanded his magnificent chest. He let it out with a triumphal whoop like a boy about to go on vacation, and added, "I have a marvelous plan."

"What is it, sir?" Jeff suddenly felt slightly nervous.

"First I have to find out if Norby's other mysterious talents work with a certain object I have in mind."

"Something in your home on Mars, Admiral?" asked Norby.

"Right," said Yobo. "Now—homeward, and then—adventure!"

2.

The Heirloom

Jeff watched in the viewscreen as the ship approached the Mars dome. It was a fantastic structure that from space looked all in one piece but was actually segmented to cover the City (there was only one and nobody called it anything else), the suburbs, and the outlying farms, which extended almost up to the polar ice caps where the dome stopped.

"There's our private dock," Yobo said proudly, pointing. He was at the controls, absorbed in the sight of his beloved native planet. "We have a great view of Olympus Mons—see how the dome is sealed around it?"

"Wonderful, Admiral," Jeff said, meaning it. The highest and widest mountain in the solar system was a sight every Mars-born human had a right to be proud of.

—Jeff [Norby spoke telepathically by touching him], do you have any idea what Yobo wants me to do and with which of my talents? I'm worried.

—I'm usually the worrier, Norby, but for once I'm not anticipating any problems. Let's just enjoy the weekend.

"Come on, boys," Yobo shouted as the ship slid into the dock. "I can hardly wait for Norby to start laying on hands."

—Laying on hands, Jeff? Aren't you worried now? Don't you think the admiral's mind is finally going around the bend?

—There's probably some sensible explanation.

But as the three went through the ship's airlock into that of the Yobo dock, Jeff did wonder a trifle about the admiral's mind and the mysterious plan hidden in it.

"My home," Yobo said, pointing below. "Known in the

7

annals of Martian architecture as a masterpiece of monumentality and grandeur."

Going down to ground level in the transparent elevator, Jeff agreed. Only one massive story of the house was seen, for like all Martian structures, most of it had to be underground, with automatic safety panels to shut off doors and windows in case something happened to the dome and its precious air.

The Yobo elevator did not arrive inside the main building but into a white-columned pavilion surrounded by the gardens. An automatic car, its top down, waited to take them to the house, but Yobo waved it away.

"I'd rather photograph as we walk through the gardens, which I miss up in Space Command," Yobo said, fiddling with the holocamera. "If I do say so myself, we Yobos have the best gardens on Mars—or anyplace else in the solar system—for the climate is perfectly controlled in our dome, compared to the inadequate domes of other colonies, and on stubbornly undomed Earth, gardens are victims of weather most of the time."

"This garden is the best I've seen," Jeff said truthfully.

"Look," Yobo said, "you'll never see a lusher display of Protea aristata."

"Proteins for aristocrats?" said Norby.

"No, you idiot robot. Those plants with needlelike leaves and magnificent red blossoms."

From visits to botanical gardens, Jeff recognized many other African plants. There were blue lilies, pink bell-like flowers, red cuplike blossoms with a white line around the middle and darker red on top, pelargonium, many kinds of variegated geraniums, and mind-boggling gladioli. Jeff began to regret that with all his travels he had never been anywhere on Earth's continent of Africa.

Norby pulled on Jeff's hand. —The admiral was wrong. His sister is home after all and doesn't look happy about us.

Above the wide black marble steps of the mansion, the

8

huge front door had opened. On the threshold stood a tall, slender woman wearing a flowing russet gown with African designs on the bodice. Unlike her brother, she had plenty of hair that was gray only at the sides. Her expression was slightly grim, but Jeff tried to be charitable.

—She's a handsome woman, Norby.

—She looks snooty.

—Just try to behave yourself.

—But I always do! When things go wrong, it's always somebody else's fault!

Jeff dropped Norby's hand and whispered to the admiral. "What's your sister's name, sir?"

Yobo waved to her. "Hi, Eevee!" In a whisper he said, "She's actually Elizabeth Victoria, but you'd better call her Mrs. Yobo, since she married a distant cousin of ours and didn't have to change her last name, not that women do these days anyway—ah, yes, Eevee? I didn't hear what you were saying."

"I said you might have let me know you were coming, Boris. And with guests." She looked down her nose at Jeff and Norby.

"I did send a message, Eevee. To the butler, because I thought you'd be working."

"This is a three-day holiday even for lawyers," said Eevee. "And sending a message to our butler was useless because it is in the repair shop. Robots are impossibly unreliable."

"Not me," said Norby," "I'm always reliable. Almost."

"That will do, Norby," said Yobo. "Eevee, this is Cadet Jefferson Wells and his—um—teaching robot, Norby, who are helping me with my new holocamera this weekend. We're just stopping here for tea and to pick up something I need."

Eevee inclined her head a fraction of a centimeter. "Cadet Wells. And—robot."

Norby attempted a bow, but he tilted too far forward and

9

almost fell hat-down on Eevee's elegant toes until he turned on his miniantigrav and swung back onto his two-way feet.

"Pleased to meet you, ma'am," Norby said, deferentially touching the knob on his hat as if he were an old-time serf pulling his forelock in the presence of the aristocracy. "I'd be happy to try repairing your robot butler. I won't charge, either."

"Don't even think of it, Norby," said Yobo. "Your track record on repairing my equipment is terrible. The last time you adjusted the Space Command computers all the reports came out in Chaucerian English for days."

"I was reading *Canterbury Tales* at the time," said Norby.

"Robots!" Eevee said with a definitive, disapproving sniff that closed the conversation. With frigid courtesy she let her unexpected guests into the house.

Jeff took the little robot's hand again, to soothe his presumably outraged circuits. —Never mind, Norby. I know you're special.

—I'd like to tell her about my talents for hyperdrive and telepathy and time travel, to say nothing of how I can rescue human beings who get into trouble, as they always do.

—Don't tell anyone, Norby. Just remember that while the admiral's sister may be the most aristocratic human in the Federation, you are the most aristocratic of robots.

Jeff tried to scan the wonderful artworks as he followed Yobo through the mansion, but the number of objects was overwhelming and he was glad when they ended in the living room that was at surface level for a view of the gardens.

"Since you're in time for tea," said Eevee, poised on a couch in front of the low tea table, "I must warn you that the prime minister will be visiting—"

"The prime minister of the Federation?" Norby exclaimed.

"There is only one prime minister these days," Eevee said acerbically. "She is bringing her youngest child to meet my grandchild, Martin."

"That's my grandnephew Martin Chen," Yobo explained. "His father's a physician in the City."

"Of Oriental heritage." Eevee frowned. "I believe that his family came from someplace called San Francisco."

Jeff tried not to smile. "How old is your grandson, ma'am?" He'd decided that "ma'am" was easier than "Mrs. Yobo," and of course "Eevee" was not for anyone outside the family.

"Martin is nine," said Eevee. "Right now he's in the neighborhood playing baseball, but he should be home by the time the prime minister arrives."

"And how is Wenoa?" There was a suspiciously innocent blandness in Yobo's broad face, and Jeff was surprised that even the chief admiral of Space Command dared to refer to the prime minister by her first name.

"Boris," Eevee said with a frown, "please try not to flirt with Wenoa Grachev."

"Me? Flirt with a prime minister?"

Eevee compressed her lips, then opened them to say, "We must be careful when she tries to talk to us about family heirlooms. In her hycom call she said something about showing her daughter a particular heirloom that Wenoa, in her vast arrogance, thinks may belong to the Grachevs, or once belonged to them—I didn't understand which she meant."

Yobo chuckled. "Wenoa has always said that our families are supposed to be related."

"Bah," said Eevee, sounding remarkably like her brother. "When it comes to ancestry, Wenoa herself is simply a mongrel. Why, she's mostly old-time Russian, mixed with Welsh and Spanish and of course that Native American grandmother after whom she's named. I never approved of your dating Wenoa when you were both young."

"We're not exactly old now," Yobo said mildly, with a wink at Jeff. "Furthermore, Eevee, it is said that the glory of

11

the Terran Federation is that it recognizes and applauds the fact that all humanity is one people."

"Humph! Who said that?"

"Prime Minister Grachev, in her first speech to the Federation Parliament," Yobo said with a grin. "Perhaps she should have added, 'with certain important exceptions.' "

"Certainly," said Eevee. The automated tea cart arrived and she began to pour out, as perfectly as if she were living in the era of her famous second namesake, Queen Victoria.

Nobody had shown up by the time Eevee said, "More tea, Mr. Wells?"

"No thanks, ma'am. And please call me Jeff. I'm only a cadet at the Space Academy, and not very important."

"More cucumber sandwiches?" Eevee smiled at Jeff, and he realized that she was more than handsome. She was beautiful.

"Yes, ma'am."

"There are more scones, and more raspberry jam."

Jeff basked in the good food and the beauty of his hostess, but he was aware that Norby was jiggling impatiently and making small noises as if robots had teeth to grind.

The tea seemed to have warmed up Eevee in more ways than one, for she smiled graciously at her brother and said, "I'm glad Wenoa hasn't come to disturb us, Boris. I see you so seldom. I am *so* glad you were intelligent enough not to marry her."

"As a matter of fact," Yobo said ruefully, rubbing his bald head, "it was Wenoa who decided that I would not fit in with her political ambitions because I am too married to Space Command. She couldn't imagine me traipsing along behind an important Federation official, perhaps a prime minister."

"Could you imagine it, Boris?"

"Well, no. And now, Jeff"—he was obviously eager to change the subject—"I'm going to show you and Norby our most important family heirloom—a carved bit of elephant tusk."

Eevee shook her head. "I know you've always liked it, Boris, but don't you think our collection of antique African weaving is more impressive?" She turned to Jeff. "Some of the cloth pieces are so fine, so beautifully designed, that as works of art they belong in museums. In fact, museums have begged for them."

But Yobo had already risen and taken an object from a corner cabinet. He showed it to Jeff and Norby. "You can see that this is only the tip of an elephant tusk, cut in half, carved and polished. Our great-great-grandmother brought it to Mars when she decided to settle here after finishing her work as a cosmonaut."

A stipple pattern of dots decorated the flat side of the tusk and there were odd wavy lines on the rounded side, with what Jeff thought of as tiny squiggles carved under the lines.

"Look at the cut bottom," Yobo said. "We've always wondered whether or not that design could mean something Arabic, perhaps added later when the various cultures intermingled in Africa."

On the bottom of the piece of ivory was a carving that looked like a half-moon with possibly a star on top.

"It's very interesting, sir," Jeff said judiciously.

"Something about it bothers me," Norby said.

"What?" Yobo asked.

"I don't know, sir. Just—something."

"Keep thinking, Norby. I'm counting on you."

"Well, I was thinking, Admiral, that if your great-great-grandmother was a cosmonaut, didn't she explore with Russians, or Soviets, or whatever they were called? Exploring the solar system, I mean."

Eevee looked as if she were about to explode, so Yobo said hurriedly, "We have a standard joke in the Yobo family that great-great-grandmother wanted all the firstborn sons to have Russian names, but it probably doesn't mean anything, although of course I did get named Boris. . . ."

"My grandson is named after Martin Luther King, an ancient American, but the name is honorable," said Eevee. "If only it didn't have to be attached to 'Chen.' Really, Boris, this nonsense about Russian names in our family is a myth you should not perpetuate."

Norby reached out timidly to touch the heirloom for a second. "This has a lot of history in it, Admiral."

"Ah, good," Yobo said with immense satisfaction. "Just what I was hoping."

Jeff was trying to swallow the last of his scone in order to ask the admiral what Norby was supposed to do with this special heirloom, but he never had a chance. The living-room door opened suddenly. A thrillingly resonant, deep, but utterly feminine voice rang out.

"Boro! My heart skips beats at the sight of you! I am *sooooo* passionately pleased that you are here!"

Admiral Yobo stood up again as if pulled by wires. His sister remained seated, clamping her jaw. Norby fell off his seat next to Jeff, who had also jumped up.

—Jeff, you knocked me off! Clumsy human!

—Sorry, Norby, but everyone's supposed to stand when a prime minister enters a room.

Jeff thought that in person Wenoa Grachev was much. more than a prime minister. In a black and white outfit, she was as handsome as Elizabeth Victoria Yobo. In addition, she seemed to carry with her a supercharged atmosphere that Jeff's older brother would have recognized as sex appeal. Jeff swallowed and tried to salute.

Wenoa was as tall and graceful as Eevee, but twice as curved. She wore her ungrayed black hair in a shaggy mane that suited her personality and enhanced the strong features on her lively face. Her dark gaze seemed to penetrate into one's very bones, and Jeff felt almost sorry for the pale little girl beside her.

14

"This is my daughter, Natasha Bergaard. She uses my husband's Scandinavian name." Wenoa stroked the child's light hair and added, "We're rather pleased to have one child who's clearly a throwback to our North European ancestors."

Eevee sniffed.

The admiral cleared his throat. "Let me introduce Cadet Jefferson Wells and his robot, Norby. Of course, you already know my sister."

At this moment a little boy dashed into the room from the back way, shouting, "Sorry I'm late, Grandma, but we won the game." He skidded to a stop, smiled hastily at Eevee, and peered at Natasha.

"My grandson, Martin." Eevee gestured toward the other couch. "Do sit down, Wenoa. You're late for tea."

"Run out to the garden with Martin, Natasha," said Wenoa. When the boy led the girl out by the hand, Wenoa lowered herself onto the couch where Yobo had been sitting and pulled him down next to her. Jeff had to sit on the other couch, and could hear Norby chuckling metallically.

Suddenly Wenoa cried out. "Boris! That's our family heirloom you have in your hand!"

3.

Getting Away

"You are referring to *my* family heirloom." There was a dangerous note in Eevee's voice. "I'll have you know that the elephant tusk was handed down from tribal leader to tribal leader in ancient Africa—"

"Or so we believe." Yobo sounded apologetic.

"—and to our immediate family from the most famous Martian Yobo, our great-great-grandmother."

Wenoa took an official-looking envelope from her pocket and flourished it. "This will prove—"

"Don't wave documents at me!" Eevee did not exactly shout, but the decibels had risen. "I will not believe that my great-great-grandmother gave the Yobo ivory heirloom to a Russian cosmonaut!"

"I didn't exactly say—" Wenoa began.

"Ladies, it has been a pleasure to see both of you." Yobo rose and stuffed the ivory heirloom into the pocket of his tunic. "But I must be on my way. Come along, Norby, Jeff. We have work to do."

"But Boro, love, you must not leave!" The prime minister's long eyelashes fluttered and the Federation emblem on her tunic gyrated with her emotion. "I want to show you these documents!"

"Show them to Eevee, who will no doubt explain everything to me," Yobo said. "Eevee, thanks for tea. We'll be back before the weekend's over."

"With the *Yobo* family heirloom?"

"Certainly, certainly."

Wenoa said, "Boro, wait!" but Yobo quickly kissed her and

16

dashed out, with Jeff in tow, before he could hear what else she had to say.

The two human males and one small robot galloped to the airlock elevator, the garden passing in a blur of color. When the ship left Mars with Norby at the controls and entered hyperspace, the admiral sighed with obvious relief.

"Safe," he said, wiping his brow. "Important females bother me. Especially older and supposedly wiser women, like sisters and prime ministers."

"Is Wenoa Grachev actually older than you are?" Jeff asked as if it were an innocent question.

"Um. Politically minded females always *seem* ol—I mean wiser."

Norby winked one of his back eyes at Jeff. His front eyes were staring at the control board. "Where to, Admiral?"

"No place yet. Here, look at my heirloom again."

"It looks the same as it did on Mars."

"Yes, but now hold it again."

Norby put one metal finger on the curved side of the ivory. "I don't need to lay on my whole hand, Admiral. One finger will do if you want me to tune in to the object. But it's not mechanical or electronic, so I'm not sure what it is you want me to tune in to."

"Use all your mysterious scanning talents to tune in to the *past* of this object."

"Difficult, but not impossible," Norby said. "What for?"

"I want to take my holocamera into the past at the time this piece of ivory was still part of the whole tusk and on the actual elephant who grew that tusk."

A tiny chill trickled down Jeff's spine. "Time travel is very tricky, Admiral. And I don't see how Norby can pinpoint anything in the past like that."

"Well I can, too!" Norby squeaked metallically. "I'm a genius robot and can do almost anything. I'll find the elephant, that's for sure."

"No!" Jeff said firmly. "Time travel is dangerous."

"But only Norby can do it," said Yobo. "You've always told me that he's partly alien machinery, containing a certain bit of metal left over from a previous universe or something."

"Yes," said Jeff, "but the Others don't approve of time travel, and since Norby's special metal is the only thing in our universe that makes it possible, he and I try not to time-travel unless it's really necessary."

"The Others." Yobo tapped his chin. "If I didn't know Norby's talents, I'd be inclined to doubt your stories about that mysterious race of aliens. After all, I've never met them. Are they really so wonderful and wise?"

"They are now," said Jeff. "Their civilization is older than the entire history of Homo sapiens—or hominids, or even early primates. They've been around a long time and learned a great deal. They live only in spaceships now, and don't interfere with developing planetary civilizations."

Norby added, "You humans have graduated to orbital settlements and you've colonized some of the planets, moons, and asteroids in your solar system, but that's not much compared to a genuine space-faring people like the Others."

"Please, Admiral," said Jeff. "The Others wouldn't like it if you interfered in the time of your ancestors."

"I didn't have interference in mind," said Yobo. "Just a quick dash through time and space to a marvelous African savannah to photograph the very elephant that grew this family heirloom. We won't damage the elephant, or history, and it will be a pleasant little adventure for a long weekend."

"The whole weekend to photograph an elephant?" said Norby.

"We have to allow time for your mistakes, Norby, plus going back to Mars to show the movie—we'll tell Eevee it's an elephant *like* the one that grew the tusk, but I'll know it's the real one. What about it, Jeff? I can order you to order your robot to take the *Pride* back in time for me, but this is my purely private adventure, so I'll merely request. And don't forget that not only is the idea mine, but the entire responsibility is mine."

The trouble is, thought Jeff, that I do want to go.

—It might be fun. [Norby touched him]

"Admiral," Jeff said slowly, "it's true that time travel can be dangerous. Once Norby and I changed history rather badly when we got mixed up in eighteenth-century France* and we had to work hard to set things right, but most of the time nothing terrible happens. I don't see how recording the images of an elephant can change history."

"I can't either," said Yobo. "At that time the world was taking very little notice of what was going on in the Africa of my ancestors. But I wouldn't want Norby to tune in to the more recent past of the ivory and interfere with great-great-grandmother's—er—affairs."

"Did she really have one with that Russian cosmonaut? Is that why she decided to name her firstborn after him?" Norby asked eagerly.

Jeff was embarrassed. "Don't talk about rumors, Norby."

"But Admiral Yobo himself hints at it, don't you?"

Yobo grunted. "Eevee will have a fit if she finds out that the cadets—even one cadet—think there was some illegitimate Russian blood mixed into our ancestry."

"Perhaps," Jeff said diplomatically, "the African and Russian cosmonauts were just good friends."

"Great and good?" muttered Yobo. "Anyway, he died— an accident at the end of the Io mission. And, as my sister always points out, great-great-grandmother very legitimately married a distant relative later, one of the early Martian colonists. No doubt great-great-grandmother was merely paying tribute to a fallen comrade when she named her firstborn Boris."

"Yes, sir," said Jeff and Norby.

"Great-great-grandmother became quite important in the

*See *Norby and the Queen's Necklace.*

Mars Colony, as it was known then. She was not only responsible for making Swahili the official colony language, but she became the matriarch of the whole family. I think my sister longs to be just like her ancestor."

"Except for being very good friends with a Russian," said Norby.

Yobo patted the knob on Norby's hat. "Odd that right now there's a Russian—sort of—in Eevee's house, trying to be friends, or at least a relation. It might be amusing to think of Wenoa Grachev as a member of our snobbish Yobo family."

Jeff pointed to the heirloom. "If the prime minister thinks your great-great-grandmother gave that to a Russian member of her family, then we'd better be careful with it. Perhaps she wanted to show you a love note in which your ancestor mentions the gift."

"Don't mention the words 'love note' to my sister. It's bad enough that Wenoa's great-great-grandfather was the brother of that Russian cosmonaut . . . is something wrong, Norby?"

"I don't know." Norby was swaying back and forth with his eyes closed. They opened and he blinked at Yobo and Jeff. "I was touching the elephant tusk again and wondering if I could find it in the past. . . ."

"Wondering?" Yobo growled. "You mean you aren't certain you can find it?"

"I said I'm a genius robot. I didn't say *perfect*."

"But what happened, Norby?" asked Jeff.

"Something—don't know—odd."

"Admiral," said Jeff, "maybe this adventure is not safe."

"Then you won't order Norby to find my ancestral elephant?" Yobo asked plaintively.

"The elephant wasn't your ancestor," said Norby. "It was killed, or scavenged by your ancestors."

Yobo sighed. "Whatever. I did so want a small adventure for this long weekend. Jeff, you've had so many big adventures in your short life, at least since you bought Norby in that used-robot shop."

"I have to be back at Space Academy by the end of the weekend, Admiral, and something's bothering Norby. . . ."

"But it's only a *small* adventure! Nothing life-or-death. Just making a little movie!" Yobo glared at Norby. "Just what was bothering you, anyway? A glitch in your circuits?"

"Or was it something in the ivory?" asked Jeff.

"When I touched the heirloom, I had the feeling that the elephant was big and strong and that I sort of wanted to see it myself. I think now that something else altogether made my emotive circuits jangle a little. It couldn't have been the elephant, because it's been dead for centuries."

"What was it, then?" asked Yobo.

"As if something was trying to touch me. I wasn't paying close attention because I was trying to figure out how to get into the past very accurately—although we can always come back and try again if I miss the first time—can't we, Admiral?"

"We'll go in the ship, so we'll be safe," said Yobo. "How about it, Jeff? Aren't you tempted?"

"Yes. I've never been to Africa, past or present. And I love elephants."

Yobo smiled and said, "Then onward—"

He didn't finish, because suddenly Norby closed up completely—his domed hat slammed down on his barrel, his arms and legs withdrew inside. Only his sensor wire snaked out from the knob on his hat, full length.

"Norby!" Jeff picked up the little robot. "What is it?" There was no answer, and Jeff could make no telepathic contact.

Long minutes passed, but finally Norby's head popped up. "Stop pounding me telepathically, Jeff! I was trying to concentrate on the message."

Yobo frowned. "I thought there was no way to intercept

21

hycom messages when one is actually in hyperspace, even if the hycom transmission itself uses hyperspace."

"I've never understood that," said Jeff.

"Come to think of it, neither do I," said Yobo. "Norby, can you explain?"

"Explain hyperspace?" Norby's arms came out and he pointed to the gray nothingness that was all hyperspace showed in the viewscreen. "Perhaps Terran philosophers are correct when they say that it's best to think of hyperspace as the groundwork of the universe, the everything from which the somethings emerge—"

"Halt!" shouted Yobo. "No philosophical discourses. Tell us about the message you received."

"Oh, didn't I say? Admiral, you can speak the language of the Others, because it's the same one the Jamyn dragons use. Why don't you and Jeff just listen in?" Norby held out his hands to the two humans.

Holding Norby's hand, Jeff listened telepathically.

—I feel your presence now, Jeff, and that of someone who is strange to me.

—Rembrandt!

Norby spoke aloud, to Yobo. "He's the Other we know best, sir. Jeff named him because we can't pronounce his real name and because he's an artist."

—I am indeed the Other you know as Rembrandt, and my ship is in hyperspace near yours. We detected the entry of your ship into hyperspace, but since we did not recognize it, we tried a little mental probing to see who else had invented hyperdrive.

—It's my hyperdrive [Norby said] and this is Admiral Yobo's personal ship. We're on a mission.

—I would be honored to meet you, Admiral Yobo. I have heard so many good things of you from Jeff and Norby. Please visit my ship.

Jeff saw that the admiral seemed to be stricken dumb, until Norby kicked Yobo on the shin.

"What? Oh, yes." Yobo cleared his throat and switched to Jamyn. Jeff had forgotton to tell him that on Rembrandt's visit to Earth he had learned Terran Basic.

—I mean, sir [said Yobo] that I am even more honored to have the opportunity to meet you.

All the polite exchanges irritated Jeff, for he realized that something more important was involved. —Rembrandt, were you by any chance *trying* to reach Norby?

—Yes, I was. Didn't he tell you?

—Sorry, Rembrandt [said Norby], but in trying to engineer this small adventure of the admiral's, I wasn't paying attention to telepathic messages. It's hard to remember that unlike humans, you Others can do long-distance telepathy if you try hard enough.

—It does take considerable effort.

—Are you having a crisis? [said Norby] Something terrible that requires my help?

—No, Norby. Nothing terrible.

Rembrandt paused, as if not knowing how to proceed with the telepathic conversation.

—Something not terrible, but bad enough? [asked Norby].

—Not at all. I was just hoping that you and Jeff, and you, Admiral, if it interests you, might consent to performing a small service for us.

—Of course we will [said Norby and Jeff].

—What is it? [Yobo asked suspiciously, not knowing Rembrandt the way Jeff did].

—Perhaps I can explain better if you visit my ship, and meet my sister, who is visiting—

—Your *sister!* [That was Yobo.]

—Yes, it is she who would like you to do something for her, but we must discuss it first.

—We'll be right over, after I connect our airlocks [said Norby, blinking at an apparently aghast Yobo].

—Then good-bye for now. Please go directly to our observation lounge. My sister and I will join you there.

Yobo dropped Norby's hand and said weakly, "Jeff, you've told me so much about this wonderful Other. Why is it that you never told me he has a *sister!*"

"I didn't know he had one. But don't be upset, Admiral. She's not human. She's an alien—one of the Others. And she's probably thousands of our years old."

"Just my luck," said Yobo. "Another older woman."

4.

Another Mission

As they entered the observation lounge in the Others' ship Yobo stopped as if overwhelmed. Jeff understood, for the huge room still had the same effect on him. It was not only large, but there was a clean beauty in its curved lines, and the stern wall was all window, now showing only the gray of hyperspace.

"Admiral, when the ship is in normal space, you can see the most fantastic view—of stars, if we're in a galaxy, or of islands of them if we're between the galaxies," said Jeff.

"Between galaxies! Imagine the experiences these Others must have as they journey all over our universe!" Yobo walked to the window and touched it gently. "There's no technology in the Federation producing an optically perfect window of this size that could still withstand the stresses a hyperdrive ship has to undergo. It makes my porthole look absurd."

Jeff, Norby, and Yobo were alone in the room, and in fact had not seen anyone since they came through the two airlocks.

"There's no place to sit," said the admiral. The room was empty except for a white pedestal that held one of Rembrandt's crystal-and-light sculptures and, on a nearby wall, a large portrait of a Jamyn dragon-mother and her child.

"First look at the sculpture, Admiral," said Jeff. "You can see—or feel—I'm not sure what, but almost anything you want, or are supposed to—I don't know. . . ."

"If that's the best you can do in art appreciation, Jeff, I

wonder how you manage to pass your courses at the academy." But Yobo walked over to the sculpture and studied it.

"Like it, Admiral?" asked Norby.

"I'm not sure what I'm seeing." Yobo unconsciously echoed Jeff. "Strange—it makes me feel good, as if hope could be a permanent aspect of the universe."

Norby touched Jeff. —I'm sure that sculpture reveals what the viewer wants most. Is hope what Yobo wants?

—Perhaps hope for an interesting life. Maybe the admiral is so fanatical about his holocamera because right now he's very bored with his existence, his job at Space Command.

—Or he may be lonely. You saw how he kissed the prime minister. Judging from my observations of experts in human kissing, like your brother, I'd say the admiral's pretty good.

As if in answer to their thoughts, Yobo said meditatively, "I want more time to appreciate beauty in art and music and, um, people. Don't tell anyone, cadet, but even my job hasn't satisfied me lately."

"You're the best chief admiral the Federation has ever had," Jeff said.

Yobo shook his head and his back seemed to wilt. "Maybe, but it's not enough, is it? Don't answer that. You're only fifteen and you can't possibly know. And don't say I'm having one of those ridiculous mid-life crises, not that I'm actually in mid-life—"

"Oh, no, Admiral," said Jeff and Norby, in chorus.

"All I want is to go back to my ancestors, to find the hope that was in them, the hope and beauty that made them carve that bit of elephant tusk. I want to know what the symbols mean, what my ancestors were trying to convey."

Jeff was trying to think of something he could say to cheer up the admiral, who looked distinctly depressed, when Yobo straightened up and glared at him.

"Are these Others going to keep us standing forever?"

"Oh, I'm so sorry, Admiral," Jeff said, trying to gesture the way Rembrandt did.

"What in the universe are you doing, cadet? Making mystic passes to turn me into a chair?"

"Trying to make the floor make seats."

"Are you out of your mind?"

Norby rushed to a strange little design on the wall, near the floor. His sensor wire extruded and he plugged himself into a small hole in the center of the design.

"Has Norby gone out of his mind, too?" Yobo asked. "Or is he just recharging himself?"

"He recharges in hyperspace ordinarily, and he's done that," Jeff said, "so I don't know what he's doing. Norby?"

With a faint whispery noise, four low seats covered in shimmery gold fabric rose from the floor.

"Magic!" said Yobo.

"Advanced technology," said Norby, withdrawing his sensor wire from the wall. "I just asked Yib to provide for beings who need to sit."

"Yib?"

Jeff laughed and said, "Norby named this ship's computer 'Yib.' He says it means 'You immense brain.' Did you say hello, too, Norby? I always thought that you and Yib were sort of friendly."

"We are." Norby lowered an eyelid slightly and spoke in Terran Basic. "She's actually not too bright, but what little emotive circuitry she has is certainly in favor of me."

"Another female," Yobo muttered in the same language. "And I'm trying to find hope."

"Hope was something the universe almost didn't get, thanks to women," Norby said at his pedantic best. "I've read myths."

"Oh, you have, have you?" said Yobo. "And just what do you think women did to louse things up?"

Norby's hands moved to the middle of his barrel, jointed elbows out. He resembled a miniature fat professor about to lecture. "The Greek gods gave Epimetheus two things— Pandora, his wife, and a box they told him he shouldn't open. Naturally, being male, he obeyed and didn't open the box, but Pandora did, letting loose all the evils of the world."

"Very wrong of her," Yobo said, "but to be expected. I'm sure my sister would have done the same thing."

"They closed the box after all the evils had escaped into the world—typically human, trying to be careful when it's too late. Look how your ancestors almost ruined planet Earth before they built settlements anyplace else in the solar system! Polluting the atmosphere, ocean, and land—"

"Norby," Jeff said, "finish the myth."

"—selfishly using the wrong things that punched holes in the ozone layer, burning fossil fuels that sent out not only pollutants but carbon dioxide, and then cutting down forests that ate the carbon dioxide, so there was nearly a runaway greenhouse effect, and of course overpopulating—"

"Norby," Yobo said in an ominous rumble, "you are making me feel that when it comes to humanity, there's little hope."

"I'll finish the myth, Admiral," Jeff said before Norby had a chance. "From the closed box there came a little voice asking to be released. At first people thought it was another evil, but when the box was opened, out came fragile little hope. So from that day on, no matter how many evils there are, hope always exists."

"If we try hard," Yobo said softly, not noticing that Norby had reached out to touch Jeff.

—Jeff, in the version of the myth I read, hope remained in the box, in the control of humankind.

—I'd rather believe hope is free, for all intelligences in the universe.

Yobo lowered himself glumly to one of the seats. "Do you suppose these Others aren't showing up because they don't trust me? Or do we carry bacteria that might hurt them? Are they going to fumigate the room before they'll join us?"

"Nothing of the sort, Admiral," Jeff said, annoyed and defensive on behalf of the Others. "As I've told you, the

Others don't like to leave their ships, but Rembrandt has even visited my apartment in Manhattan.* I'm sure the Others have evolved to the point where their bodies automatically heal."

As Jeff said it, he remembered that during one of his adventures into the past, he met an Other from a much earlier time who was dying of a disease even his people could not control. "We're all healthy, Admiral. So is Rembrandt."

The door to the lounge dilated open and Rembrandt stepped through. He had only two legs and odd-looking but genuine feet, so that in spite of his four arms he seemed humanoid. Below his hairless scalp his face was almost human, with an expression of goodness and friendliness that you couldn't help liking, even if he did have three eyes.

"Greetings," Rembrandt said in Terran Basic. "I'm sorry to be so late in meeting you, but my sister is very shy."

"Shy, eh?" Yobo looked hopeful.

"And you must be the famous Admiral Boris Yobo. I see that you share the characteristic masculinity of the Others."

Yobo's jaw dropped until he saw Rembrandt pointing to his own bald head. "A far superior way to spend adult life, don't you agree, Rembrandt?"

As the two bald males smiled at each other in the fullness of their pride, Jeff found himself wishing that his own hair was not so thick and unruly and in need of trimming.

"I don't have hair, either," said Norby.

"No, indeed," said Rembrandt. "Welcome to the club, as I believe you Terrans would put it."

"I've been admiring your artwork, Rembrandt," Yobo said.

"I would like to show you what I'm working on, but it's only just begun. I'm experimenting with a clay that when magnetized, moves in patterns you control with your mind.

*See *Norby Down to Earth.*

29

I have a new—ah—paintbrush that functions in a similar way, but I need practice before I'll dare use it."

Suddenly the door dilated again and someone stopped on the threshold, silhouetted against the stronger light of the hall beyond. The outline of the head was fuzzy, not clear-cut, and judging from the distance between the head and the top of the doorway, this Other was about the size of a medium human.

"Come in," Rembrandt said in Jamyn, adding a name that Jeff despaired of pronouncing. "Meet my friends Jeff Wells of Earth, his robot Norby, and Admiral Boris Yobo of Mars."

She seemed to glide toward them, although she had feet just like Rembrandt's, visible under the long hem of her iridescent green gown.

"Welcome." Her voice rippled like quiet music.

Jeff thought Rembrandt's sister was one of the loveliest creatures he'd ever seen, and already today he'd been captivated by the beauty of two other women.

She was not bald. Her scalp, neck, and shoulders were covered with feathery stuff like the down of a silvery baby bird. Her small face resembled Rembrandt's, equally smooth and three-eyed, but she seemed innocent, helpless, and as young as the dawn.

This time Boris Yobo did not rise as if jerked upward by wires, but slowly, as if under hypnosis. When the female Other lifted one of her lower hands to him, he held it delicately and kissed it lingeringly.

"I hope that one of you Terrans will give me a name you can pronounce," said the female Other with a radiant smile.

"Let me," Yobo said huskily, as though he were barely daring to breathe. "Your name should be that of the Greek goddess Euterpe. Her name means 'she who gladdens.' "

"I am honored. Did she sing?"

"She was the ancient goddess of lyric song."

—Jeff [said Norby], I think she should be Pandora.

—What's the matter, Norby. Don't you trust beautiful females?

—I worry about Yobo. He's worse than your brother.

Rembrandt gestured and a table rose from the floor. "We will have refreshments, if you'd like. My sister is visiting my ship so we can compare our latest creations. She lives in a ship devoted to the musical arts."

"Then, like the goddess Euterpe, you are a singer also?" Yobo goggled at her as if unable to believe she was real.

"I will sing for you if you wish." Sitting, she gestured to the floor and up popped a small cabinet from which she took what looked like an ancient lyre, except that it had more strings and was shaped like a bent diamond.

Rembrandt touched Jeff. —My sister is usually too shy to sing for strangers. Your admiral is having a remarkable effect upon her.

Odd but nourishing food came in on a mobile tray, but for once Jeff—who enjoyed what the Others ate—paid no attention to it. His gaze was fixed on Euterpe as she plucked at the lyre's strings with her upper hands and with her lower hands pressed tiny levers at the pointed ends of the diamond. When she began to sing, Jeff wanted the song to last forever.

—She's dangerous, Jeff!

—Is that you, Rembrandt?

—I'm Norby! Rembrandt's eating. This female has Yobo hypnotized. He looks as if he'd do anything she asks.

—She's so wonderful, Norby.

—Jeff, she's too old for you and not even your species.

—I know. That doesn't matter. Nothing matters except the song.

The music stopped and Jeff felt bereft. "Please sing some more, Euterpe—ma'am."

She turned to Yobo. "That was my own composition, but I would like you to hear how I've used music from your solar system. Your radio, television, and holov programs have entertained us for years. I'm enchanted by human music."

"Enchanting," said Yobo, leaning toward her like a sunflower toward the sun.

—Jeff, eat some food. You're a growing boy and you need your strength and you've only had one of Eevee's Victorian teas, not a proper lunch.

—Norby, stop nagging me. All right, I'll eat a little.

Jeff managed to eat while the fascinating Euterpe played and sang what sounded like a musical essay on the evolution of human music from every part of Earth. He could pick out Bach, Beethoven, Gershwin, Boulez, the famous Ying of the previous century, and somebody whose latest symphony was supposed to be a masterpiece, only Jeff couldn't remember her name.

Gradually Jeff became aware that more music was filling the room than that produced by Euterpe's voice and fingers.

"That was Yib playing along," Norby said when the piece ended, except that for Jeff it did not end. He thought it just stopped, and should have gone on.

Euterpe nodded. "I have taught Yib, as you call our computer, all the music I know. She contributes to this composition, which pays tribute to human music in all its tremendous diversity."

"Was that really the end of the composition?" Jeff asked.

"The end will come only when human history stops, and I hope that will not be until the universe itself grows old and dies. I and the Others after me will study human music all our lives, for there is much to learn from it."

"It was beautiful," said Yobo, "but you began it too late in time. You should go back to include the music of human cultures mistakenly called primitive because they were not technologically advanced. They were fully civilized in language, art, poetry, and music—and much of their music has been recorded and studied."

"You understand!" Euterpe leaned toward him eagerly. "I

am trying to incorporate such music into my composition, but I would like to know much earlier music from the time before humans recorded it, or even wrote it down. On your planet, humans invented music, did they not?''

"Oh, no," Jeff said, forgetting to be polite. "Many birds sing complicated songs, and so do whales."

"But she's right, Jeff," Yobo said, still staring raptly at Euterpe. "Only humans, and perhaps earlier hominids, had the intelligence to make up many different songs to convey complicated symbolism and meanings."

"I think whales do, too," Jeff said stubbornly.

"Furthermore," Yobo said, glowering at Jeff, "we humans are the most inventive. Chimpanzees, our closest relatives, use rough tools of twigs and leaves and stones but Homo habilis was the first to manufacture a permanent tool when he shaped stones. And the first to manufacture musical instruments was Homo sapiens sapiens!"

"That's your and Jeff's species," Rembrandt said with a twinkle of amusement in his three eyes. "Please eat, Admiral."

Yobo stared at the purple liquid and blue cakes as if any kind of food didn't measure up. "Music is known to us as the food of love," he muttered, but Euterpe handed him a plate of cakes and he sampled them.

"I wish," Euterpe said, "that you humans could go back in time to record early Terran music for me."

"Ah," Yobo said, beaming, "is that the service you wish me to perform for you? Because the answer is yes."

"Wait," Rembrandt said, holding up both lower hands. "I have been arguing with my sister about this. We Others long ago got rid of the metal that makes time travel possible. It is too dangerous. Only Norby has the ability now, and as I understand it, his time-travel adventures were not done for frivolous reasons."

"Seeking the history of music is not frivolous," Euterpe said, her voice like sharp ice. Suddenly she sounded to Jeff

33

like Wenoa Grachev and Eevee Yobo rolled into one. "You are one kind of artist, brother, and I am another. I do not ask that our guests do anything dangerous to themselves or to the history of their species."

Rembrandt shrugged. "Are musicians this stubborn in your solar system?"

"It is not possible to refuse a musician so beautiful," Yobo said, making it sound as if he were a medieval knight sent on a quest by his queen. "We are going back in time anyway, to photograph an animal important in the history of the Yobos. In our ship we will hover on antigrav at night, recording the music sung in the village of my ancestors."

"The prospect of hearing it delights me," Euterpe said.

—We're in for it, Jeff [Norby said]. Do your best to get the admiral out of here before we have to stay for another meal or your long weekend will be almost over before we've begun the work those two have cut out for us. For *me*.

5.

Into the Past

Back in his ship, Yobo couldn't seem to stop talking about Euterpe. "Marvelous woman. Marvelous. Blast—I meant to describe elephants to her, although she's probably seen images of them from the electronic beams we've been sending into space for centuries."

"And she's been watching them for *centuries*, Admiral," Norby added, nudging Jeff.

Yobo dismissed this with a wave of his hand. "I wanted to explain to her that the African elephant, *Loxodenta africana*, is the largest species of land animal alive on Earth. Jeff, I bet you don't know what the second largest species is."

"The hippopotamus?"

"Wrong, cadet. Not quite to the bottom of the class, however, because hippos are the third largest land animal. The second largest is the Asian elephant, *Elephas maximus*. Most people forget that the two elephants are different species."

"The news thrills me," said Norby. "Now give me that ivory heirloom of yours if you want me to tune in to the whereabouts of the elephant that grew it."

"Be careful, Norby," Jeff said, while inside he was getting more excited at the prospect of seeing a genuine wild African elephant. He'd only seen them in zoological parks.

"Hurry up," said Yobo, fingering a tiny device fastened to the simple African tunic he was now wearing. "I'm sure we can't change history taking pictures or recording music with these handy little gadgets Euterpe gave us. Amazing—they automatically record any music. We'll have to be careful

35

about bursting into our own Space Command songs. Especially some of the nonofficial ones you cadets like."

Jeff grinned. "Suppose your ancestors turn out to be terribly wild—and cannibals?"

"*My* ancestors? Eat *people?*" Yobo looked on the verge of an explosion until it came out in a big guffaw. "Hah! I'm too big to fit in any pot, and I'll give them trouble if they try to cut me up. Norby can always escape on antigrav—"

"And I'll take both of you with me, but remember that if we have to go into hyperspace, or above the atmosphere, my personal protective field won't hold more than one of you."

"We won't need it," Yobo said. "If we're seen by my ancestral tribe, I'll pretend to be a traveling magician with a magic barrel that does tricks—"

"Admiral!" Norby squeaked in agitation. "We shouldn't let anyone even see us if we can avoid it!"

"—and Jeff can be a slave I captured in my travels far to the north."

"Oh, great," Jeff mumbled. I hope this is just a *little* adventure, he said to himself, again.

"How do you know you've gone back in time as well as space, Norby?" Yobo peered out of the porthole. Planet Earth was beautiful from space, but the side they were looking at was wreathed with cloud, so it was hard to tell what was below.

"I just know I've gone back, that's all."

"There's a continent!" Jeff yelled. "Africa, Europe—we're on the correct side of the Atlantic, and the landmasses seem the same shape as in our day, so we haven't gone too far back in time, when they were all jammed together in Pangea, before humans existed."

"But Norby," Yobo said, "how do you know you've moved back far enough in time?"

"I'm an efficient genius. Usually. Besides, when we came

36

out of hyperspace, it was on the dark side of the planet. Did you see any lights anywhere?"

"You're right," said Yobo. "Excellent, Norby. This means that my ancestral elephant lived at a time when my tribe was young, obviously before electric light was invented further north. The Yobos are an ancient family. Great-great-grand-mother was said to be particularly proud of her heritage from tribal kings. Let's go down to Africa now."

"We can't find your elephant that way," Norby said. "I must tune in to the heirloom again. If that tusk exists on Earth right now, I ought to feel a tremendous pull on the heirloom, trying to get to itself. I'll follow the pull until the heirloom melts into the actual tusk the elephant is presuma-bly wearing at the moment."

"How will I get the heirloom back again!" Yobo looked horrified. "I never thought you'd have to do it that way! Eevee will kill me if I don't bring back the heirloom. And then there's Wenoa—if she's got a letter proving that her great-great-granduncle was given our heirloom, then I may have to give it to her."

"The heirloom might reappear of its own accord once we leave this time period," Norby said.

"But it might not?"

"Time-travel paradoxes are peculiar. I've never understood them, in spite of my genius."

Yobo groaned. "I'll have to rethink this whole thing."

Jeff touched Norby. —This is going to ruin the admiral's weekend. Can't we do something to satisfy him?

Norby took the heirloom from Yobo and held it for a minute. Then he handed it back. "Is there a small stasis box on the ship?"

"I think so."

"Let's put the heirloom in the stasis box, to stay in the ship. I think I have a fix on the elephant now, sir, and will go down with your holocamera."

Yobo found the box, laid the bit of tusk reverently inside, closed the lid, and put it in the control-room safe.

—Norby, there's no guarantee the admiral's heirloom won't disappear the closer we get to the elephant.

—I know, but it's the best I can do, Jeff. And if the heirloom was going to disappear in the elephant's time period, it should have gone by now. Unless this isn't the right time.

"There," Yobo said. "Now we're ready. Hyperjump from here to Earth's lower atmosphere, and then position the ship on antigrav, over the elephant. Maybe the creature will think we're another cloud and pay no attention."

The view of distant Earth vanished, replaced by the gray of hyperspace, which almost immediately changed to a different gray that was obviously thick cloud.

"Ideal for hiding the ship," Norby said. "I feel the elephant very near."

Yobo strapped the holocamera on himself. "I can hardly wait to take my movie."

"I don't think you should go, Admiral," Jeff said, feeling oddly apprehensive. "Norby can photograph the elephant with far less danger."

"I want to take the pictures myself, and not through the porthole with a telephoto lens. I want to breathe the same air as my ancestors, even smell that elephant!"

"But Admiral . . ."

"Humor me, Jeff. Just because you don't care about your ancestors—"

"Mine are too mixed up to sort out," Jeff said. "Can't we all go? Let Norby hold you around the chest and I'll hang on to your legs. I have one of Euterpe's recording devices, too, so it will be a fail-safe way of bringing music back for her, if we hear any. At least we'll get the trumpeting of the elephant, and the way their stomachs rumble."

"Very funny." Yobo clapped Jeff on the back. "You're just

so excited about this adventure that you don't want to stay behind. Is that it, cadet?",

"Sure, Admiral." It was partly true, but mostly Jeff felt he had to take care of Yobo, who was behaving like a boy too caught up in enthusiasm to worry.

"Okay, then," Yobo said, heading for the airlock. "But don't waggle me about in the air. This camera takes holo-images in tiny fractions of a second, but I suppose if you squirm enough you'll mess up my movie. Now come on, you two. I want to see my elephant."

First Norby took Yobo out of the airlock and dangled him on antigrav so that Jeff could grab his legs.

"We must be a hilarious sight," said Yobo.

"Then let's hope the clouds stay around us until we find the elephant," said Norby.

It was impossible to see anything. Norby descended slowly as if feeling his way toward the goal of the ivory tusk. Jeff felt as if they were moving through thick soup.

"I think I sense the elephant," Norby said, "or rather the tusk. Your heirloom, Admiral, in the state of nature, so to speak. It's right about . . . oops!"

"Hey!" yelled Jeff. "I just hit the ground, hard."

"Let go of my legs, Jeff, so I can get down."

Jeff let go of Yobo and stood up, helping the admiral make a smoother landing on the Earth than he had.

"Where is my elephant?" Yobo said. "I can't see a blasted thing in this rain."

"You won't be able to photograph, will you?" asked Jeff. "Should we go away and come back in a week—"

"I don't have a week. I have a long weekend, cadet."

"I mean, Norby can take us through time, immediately."

"Ah yes, so he can, cadet, but this camera will photograph through rain if I adjust this little thing here—there—I'll take a few artistic shots through the wet and then we'll come back to photograph in the sunlight. I'll concentrate on long shots of scenery then . . . do you hear something?"

"Thunder?" asked Jeff, for there was a rumbling that sounded near. "But I didn't see any lightning. . . ."

As if nature had heard, there was a flash of light that turned the molten lead color of the rain to shining silver, and somebody screamed. The sound was followed at once by a crash of thunder that seemed to shake the ground.

Jeff had been staring right at Yobo and Norby, and knew they hadn't screamed. Whoever did it was behind him.

"Jeff," Yobo said, "turn around. Right behind you—I saw a small child coming toward us, only the lightning blinded me, so that it's hard to see anything now except this awful rain. And we're on the day side of the planet, too."

Jeff turned and dimly saw what looked like the form of a small child stumbling along through the pelting rain. The child was crying bitterly, as if not only frightened by the storm but hurt. In fact, the child seemed to be limping.

"Here!" Jeff called. "Come to us!"

The ominous rumble came again and the child limped faster, but not fast enough. Lightning flared, and silhouetted against it was an enormous shape, coming after the child as the thunder boomed again.

"It's your elephant, Admiral!" Norby shouted. "Use your holocamera!"

Jeff, closer to the child, tried to get to it, but he slipped in the wet grass and fell. Horrified, he saw the tusks of the beast smash against the child's body, hurling it to one side.

Yobo ran faster than Jeff had thought possible. He picked up the child and ran back to Norby.

"Get up, Jeff! We've got to get out of here!" Yobo shouted. "Norby—help Jeff. . . ."

It was too late. Jeff was on his feet, but before he could run or before Norby could take him away, he heard an unmistakable trumpeting. Through the rain, something immense loomed over him and a long trunk wound around his body.

Before he could cry out, Jeff was lifted off his feet and pulled back toward the huge head, the breath of the creature hot upon him, the two tusks walling him on either side.

6.

Disaster

The rain was pouring down Jeff's face, into his eyes and ears, but he heard Norby.

"I'm coming, Jeff. I'll get you out." Norby hovered on antigrav, trying to pull him away from the trunk. When it held firm, Jeff let go of Norby.

"My arm will come out of its socket," he managed to say.

Norby pushed out his sensor wire. "I'll see if I can give this monster an electric shock," Norby said. "I'm not equipped to do much damage that way, but I'll try. The sensation might persuade it to drop you."

"Hurry! It's squeezing me, and I don't like the look in its eyes."

Norby came down and shocked the tip of the trunk. The beast squealed like a stuck pig but the trunk did not unwind.

"Hit it, Norby!" Yobo shouted. "Hit it and shock it at the same time!"

Norby zoomed in, aiming at the massive head behind Jeff, but the creature seemed to explode with its own sound of thunder, deep in its throat. Its head shook and the huge tusks went up, the ivory point of one of them crashing upon Norby's metal body with a noise like a drum suddenly shattered.

The tip of the curved tusk broke off, falling back on Jeff, landing on his chest. His hand closed around the blunt, broken end, and without consciously deciding to do so, he used the piece of tusk like a dagger, stabbing again and again at the thick trunk that held him.

Norby came back again on his antigrav, hovering in the

rain over Jeff. He pulled at Jeff's other arm, and then on his shoulders, but the trunk's grip was too strong.

Jeff stabbed at the trunk with the creature's own tusk point, but it didn't seem to dent the thick skin that seemed curiously wiry and slippery in the rain.

Lightning flashed again; thunder rumbled—and so did the beast holding Jeff, who hoped it wouldn't think about throwing its trunk up and then smashing its human victim upon the nearest rock.

"Do something, Norby!" Yobo's voice was authoritatively loud, even if Jeff couldn't see him.

"I'm trying! Jeff, I think I'll have to lift this monster up on antigrav, and then drop him so he'll let go of you."

"You can't—it'll break the legs of Yobo's ancestral elephant!" Jeff shouted back, except that it was hard to shout because the trunk was squeezing his chest. Worse, he could hardly see Norby because it was now raining harder.

"Norby!" shouted Yobo. "Save Jeff! This child is badly hurt, bleeding—I think it's a little girl. Kill the elephant if you have to."

"I have the admiral's permission to kill it, Jeff, but I'm not sure I'll be able to catch you before you hit the ground with the elephant, so first I'll try dropping my body on its head, and if that doesn't knock it out, I'll take both of you to a nice zoo in our own time where they can tranquilize it without hurting it . . . except that it'll be dead, because it won't fit in my protective field when we go through hyperspace, so I'd better try killing it here."

"Norby! Stop talking and save Jeff!" Yobo shouted.

As Norby flew upward to let gravity help him fall harder, the beast was snorting and making the loud rumbling sound they had all heard before. It also kept swinging Jeff up and down, hitting him on the ground each time. With each swing, Jeff saw that the thick legs were moving forward, toward Yobo.

Jeff saw Norby hurtle down through the rain and hit the

head of the beast, but it was only enraged, not hurt enough to let go. "Take my hand, Norby. Try again to get me out of the trunk, and if you can't, you'll have to lift both of us up and drop us—not far enough to kill either of us, but enough to stun the elephant."

Norby's hand found his, but there was no way to get out of the grasp of the trunk. Jeff got a glimpse of the creature's angry, veiled eyes, and remembered that proboscideans have long eyelashes. This one did not look beautiful with long lashes, just wild with rage.

The brightness of lightning suddenly sliced through the rain-dark atmosphere, and Jeff, holding helplessly to Norby with one hand and the ivory tusk point with the other, saw Yobo just in front of them, holding the limp body of the child.

"I don't know whether my antigrav's strong enough to lift this monster," Norby said. "I'm having trouble, and I can't seem to find the ears."

"Norby!" Yobo yelled. "Stop trying that technique. Come here and make the loudest noise you can while waving your arms and legs in midair."

"Admiral—the elephant is headed in your direction! You'll be trampled! Run while you can!" Jeff shouted.

The admiral stood his ground while Norby let go of Jeff and flew there. "Yell, blast you!" said Yobo.

Since Norby's head and hands and feet were both two-way, he didn't need to turn around but immediately started flapping his arms and legs and emitting a deafening, high-pitched screeching sound.

Jeff and Yobo yelled, too, and the creature came to a halt, but the coils around Jeff tightened until he thought he couldn't breathe.

For a moment everything seemed petrified, like a fantastic tableau that Jeff was viewing through sheets of water. Gasping, he stabbed at his captor again.

All at once he heard an awesome sound and looked up to

see Yobo saying, at the top of his lungs, "Now hear this!" It had never failed to send terror into the hearts and minds of Space Cadets and everyone working in Space Command.

Yobo handed the child to Norby and advanced in the rain toward Jeff.

"Be careful, Admiral!" Jeff could speak only in a croaking whisper.

"Boooo!" Yobo shouted, waving his arms as if he were semaphoring attack plans.

As Jeff felt himself being carried backward three slow steps, Yobo strode forward. "Now hear this!" he yelled again, and followed it up with a roar that sounded worse than any of the African lion sounds Jeff had ever heard on the admiral's famous collection of wildlife recordings.

The trunk unwound around Jeff, dropping him to the ground. He rolled over in time to see the huge body of the creature moving backward in the rain, but still watching them.

"You all right, Jeff?" asked Yobo.

"Yes, sir. Thanks. You do lions well."

"I hope my ancestors are proud of me. What's that you've got in your hand?"

"The tusk point. I was using it as a dagger."

"The tusk point! The *same* tusk point?"

Jeff looked at it. "I don't know. How can we know?"

"Blast it, cadet, my ancestors were supposed to kill that animal, or at least find this tusk."

"Admiral, Jeff!" Norby flew toward them in the rain. "This child is unconscious. I think she's dying."

"Was she supposed to?" asked Yobo. "Perhaps she'd already been hurt by the beast and we just happened along to interrupt. And in real history she died."

Jeff could see the back of the child's head, covered with wet brown hair. The rest of her was obscured by strange brown clothing that was soaked with rain and blood. She was so small that she must have learned to walk only recently.

"We can't let her die," Jeff said. "We have to take the chance that it might change history. Do you have a first-aid kit in your ship, Admiral?"

"Yes, but not for anything as bad as this. If Norby takes us all to the ship and then we go to get help, the child may die before we find a doctor."

"It would be better if Norby took her directly to Rembrandt," Jeff said. "The Others are supposed to be expert healers, for all species. He'll know what to do for her, I hope. And Norby can bring her back here at the same time that he left—that is, just after. Then we'll take her to her people and we can go home."

"Why to Rembrandt? Why not to the doctors at Space Command?" Yobo asked.

"Then they'll know I can time-travel," said Norby. "Rembrandt already knows."

"Besides," said Jeff, "Space Command may want to keep her, and Norby should bring her back as soon as she's well."

"I'm sure I can bring her back to the exact instant that I left. That way, you two won't be in any danger."

"Okay, Norby. Hurry!" Jeff waved to the little robot and watched him disappear, replaced by another lightning flash. The crash of thunder seemed much later this time, and not as loud.

"The storm's abating," Yobo said. "Wish I knew where that elephant went to. Let's go look for him."

"I didn't like him at all, Admiral. And his trunk was terribly scratchy."

"But I didn't even get a good look at my own ancestral elephant!"

"I think we should stay right here and wait for Norby to come back."

"If your precious robot were as efficient as he says he is, he should have been back *now*."

45

Yobo was right. Jeff began to worry. "What if Rembrandt couldn't help because the child is dead?"

"But whatever happens to the child, Norby should come back to us." Yobo peered through the rain that was now a hazy drizzle. "Where is he!"

Suddenly the ground seemed to shake, and not from thunder. Jeff turned around and froze, for he finally saw the animal clearly for the first time, and it was running fast right toward him.

"Jeff! Run this way!"

He turned back and tried to run, but something scooped him up like snow in a snow shovel. The curved ivory tusks tossed him back onto the black trunk that did not coil around him this time, but slammed his body into the air.

He fell back on the one tusk that still had a sharp point. Trumpeting, the beast surged forward, brushing Yobo out of the way as if he weighed nothing.

Jeff's thigh felt as if he'd been speared. He tried to slide off the tusk to the ground, until he realized the huge feet would trample him to death. Instead, he held on, until the beast trumpeted, stopped short, and tossed Jeff away as if it were getting rid of worthless garbage.

Jeff turned over and over in the air, yet he seemed to be going down. The only thing he could think of was that he'd been thrown over a cliff and would painfully die on sharp rocks or branches. Instead, he hit cold water that quickly closed over his head.

7.

The Village

In spite of the terrible pain in his thigh, he swam upward, breaking the surface of the water to find that he was in a slowly moving river, close to the near shore. He was lucky, for the river had undercut the low cliff, so that he'd fallen in water, not on land. The rain had finally stopped, the sky was clearing, and there was even the beginning of a rainbow arching across the far bank of the river.

"Jeff! I'm coming!"

He looked up to see Yobo standing above him on the cliff. "I'll try to get down there, Admiral," he said, pointing further downstream, where the bank was lower and there was shoreline to crawl out on.

He tried kicking, but his leg hurt too much, so he floundered in the water, flailing his arms with difficulty until he noticed that he was still holding the broken piece of tusk in one hand.

"No, Jeff! Don't swim downriver! Wait!" Yobo leapt off the cliff, landing in the river near Jeff and nearly drowning him with the wave he made.

Jeff was sinking under the surface again, yet he held on to the tusk. Somehow he couldn't drop it in the river, even to save his own life. It felt as if the piece of ivory was a mysterious link to his own world.

Yobo reached Jeff, pulled him up, and promptly turned over. On his back, Yobo put one arm around Jeff and used his legs and his other arm to propel them both upstream.

They came to rest a short distance away, at a smooth edge of ground that sloped up to a narrow, flat ridge along the bottom of the cliff. It looked as if a path zigzagged to the top of the cliff from there.

"Downstream's no good," Yobo said, hauling Jeff onto the flat ridge. "That's where the herd comes to drink. In the storm, we must have blundered onto their path and made the leader angry. I guess the child was lost in the hard rain and had the same trouble."

Jeff almost forgot his pain when he looked downstream and saw the big bodies of the herd walking ponderously down a path of their own, wide and well-worn. The adults trumpeted to scare away a flock of ducks, while the youngsters pushed ahead to the river, sucking the water into their trunks and squirting it down their throats.

"Admiral, the river was too cold, and those elephants don't look right . . ."

"That Norby of yours should have been back long ago," Yobo muttered. "But don't worry, Jeff, I'll take care of you."

"Admiral! Look at those elephants—they have long hair—and they aren't shaped right . . ."

"Don't worry about the elephants, Jeff. Are you badly hurt? Did you land on anything in the river—some of the fish look pretty big."

"My thigh—I think I've been gored." Jeff found himself pointing with the broken tusk, and managed to laugh. "I didn't let go of it, Admiral. Maybe it's your heirloom."

Yobo grunted and tore Jeff's pant leg until the wound was easily seen. "No arterial blood, Jeff. But it's quite a gash, so I'd better tie it up. Give me that tusk."

Jeff handed it over and Yobo used it to tear a hole in the bottom of his long African tunic, made of cotton and even thinner than the clothes Jeff was wearing for Africa. The cloth tore easily all around the tunic bottom, and Yobo tied up Jeff's thigh. The makeshift bandage was soon red with blood.

"That's the best I can do for now," Yobo said. "We'll go up to the village."

48

"Village!"

"Before I jumped into the river I saw a group of huts a short distance from here, upriver. The natives must have built them on a higher rise in the land so they'd have a good view of the herds, and still be close to water. This is their path."

Jeff felt distinctly woozy. "I'm not sure I can walk up the cliff path."

"No need. I'll carry you."

"But Admiral, I'm tall—"

"And skinny. Relax. There's now a welcoming committee up there." With remarkable gentleness, and before Jeff could object again, Yobo lifted him carefully, took a deep breath, and started up the zigzag.

At first Jeff couldn't see the top of the cliff because there were too many scrubby trees in the way. He could, however, look across the river. The land undulated like a hilly prairie, as far as Jeff could see. And on that land moved great herds of animals.

"Over there it looks like Nebraska must have before the Europeans arrived," said Jeff. "I don't see the people over here—oh! Yes, I do now. Admiral—this is wrong. . . ."

"Jeff, don't worry about it." Yobo stopped and said, "Can you reach into my tunic pocket and take out that tusk? It's digging into me."

Jeff did, holding the piece of ivory close to his chest.

"If that's my heirloom," Yobo said bitterly, "it's already been paid for in your blood. I should never have let you come along on this foolhardy venture."

Carrying long spears, at least ten people waited for Yobo on the cliff top. All were dressed in leather leggings and tunics decorated with ivory beads. They wore soft leather boots tied with leather thongs, and their heads were bare in air that seemed chilly to Jeff.

"Admiral—" Jeff whispered, although it was obvious that the people would not understand what he said. "Look at

49

their skin, and their long hair! Some of them are blond, and redheaded!"

"Greetings," said Yobo in Terran Basic. "We come in peace and friendship."

The people said nothing, but tilted their spears toward Yobo as he arrived at the cliff top, panting. Several of the men were fully as tall as Yobo, and they all looked like world-class athletes. They also looked angry.

"They've probably been trying to find the lost child," muttered Yobo. "If they're angry enough—and me without a weapon, except for that tusk."

"These aren't Africans," Jeff said, feeling faint and very stupid. "Where are we?"

Yobo did not answer. He nodded to the people and said, "My friend is wounded, please help us." He said it in pleading tones, and managed to point to the blood-soaked bandage on Jeff's thigh.

At that, the people murmured among themselves, and the oldest gestured toward Yobo, saying something in a language Jeff had never heard.

"Sorry, I don't speak that," Yobo said in apologetic tones, "but please help us anyway."

The oldest walked forward, erect and proud. Her gray hair was bound back by a thin piece of leather that not only had beads on it, but tiny shells as well. She was tall, and her blue eyes gazed down at Jeff's thigh solemnly. Then she touched Yobo's cheek with a puzzled expression on her strong, lined face.

"I guess these people have never seen anybody who looks like me," Yobo said.

She looked into Jeff's face, touched his hair, and said a two-syllable word as if asking a question.

Jeff did not know what to say, but just smiled feebly at the woman. This time she caressed his wet, curly brown hair and smiled at him.

50

"I don't know what she thinks of me," Yobo said, "but apparently you'll do."

Suddenly the woman's face hardened. She pointed to the broken tusk in Jeff's hand and said something that sounded like an inquiry.

Not quite knowing why, Jeff held the tusk out to her, blunt end first. She took it, turned it over and over, and then nodded.

"Perhaps even weird strangers are acceptable if they bear gifts," Yobo said softly. "And I hope up-and-down nodding means approval here, too."

Jeff felt weaker, and as if he couldn't make his mind work properly. "But where *is* here?"

"I'll explain later, Jeff. Just relax."

The woman smiled again, stepped back to the line of spear carriers, and beckoned to Yobo.

"Well, we might as well go with them," Yobo said, marching forward with Jeff in his arms. He followed the people along the top of the riverbank that led to a higher rise in the land where there was a semicircle of large, rounded huts like brown igloos. Near the huts there were more people, including young women and children.

As Yobo plowed toward the tiny village, Jeff thought that in spite of the cool air, it must be summer, for the grass was full of flowers—red poppies and yellow buttercups and weedier plants with silver leaves and tiny yellow-green blossoms, buzzing with insects. Birds chirped and sang, and everywhere the fresh rain suddenly sparkled as the sun came out. The air smelled delicious, especially since the odor of roasting meat wafted toward Jeff.

"I feel as if I'm in a dream, Admiral. Is it real?"

"Afraid so, Jeff."

"Why are the people white?"

"Try not to worry, Jeff."

"I didn't imagine that the elephants had long hair and small ears and humps on their backs and curved tusks?"

51

Yobo sighed. "No, son. We're not in Africa, but much further north, and longer ago."

"And the elephants are not elephants but woolly mammoths?"

"*Mammathus primigenius.* When I was young and in love with Wenoa Grachev, she was so interested in ice-age art that she made me study paleolithic archaeology. Never thought I'd get here, or that my so-called family heirloom would be a piece of tusk that broke off when the elephant—I mean the big bull mammoth—hit Norby's barrel."

"Do you suppose Norby was damaged and that's why he can't get back to us?"

"I don't know, son. We're nearly at the village. Do your best to smile charmingly. That old woman seems to be important, and although she can't make head or tail of me, fortunately she seems to like you."

"I don't understand about your heirloom," Jeff said, trying to grasp what had happened, although it was so hard to think clearly.

"If that piece of tusk is my heirloom, it means that Wenoa Grachev's great-great-granduncle, the Russian cosmonaut, gave it to my great-great-grandmother, and not vice versa. Eevee will be most displeased."

"Maybe this is North America, Admiral. The prime minister had a Native American grandmother, and the way these people are dressed . . ."

"No, Jeff. We're in eastern Europe. There weren't any blond, blue-eyed Native Americans. Does your leg hurt a lot?"

"Not much." Jeff could feel the blood still seeping out. "Thanks for rescuing me, sir."

"What we need now is Norby."

"Maybe he'll come soon. . . ." Jeff's voice died away and he had trouble keeping his eyes open. He felt as if he were a little boy again, carried in the strong arms of his father.

"My father died when I was ten," he found himself mumbling.

"What's that?" asked Yobo.

Jeff could no longer remember exactly what his father looked like. He managed to open his eyes and saw Yobo's broad face peering down at him with concern.

"I'll be okay, Father. Don't worry."

"Certainly, certainly." Yobo's dark eyes seemed suddenly filmed with moisture. "Harrumph!"

Jeff smiled and lost consciousness.

8.

Surgery

When Jeff woke he was still outdoors, in the sunlight, but he was flat on his back on what felt like a thick pile of hides, gazing up at a brilliant blue sky.

Then he saw that Yobo was sitting near his head, staring down toward Jeff's legs. Jeff followed his gaze until he came to the old woman, kneeling beside his injured thigh. She was pushing a thick thread into the hold of a pointed ivory needle.

"What's she going to do!"

"Hold still, Jeff. Your thigh wound has to have a stitch in it so it won't bleed so much and will start to heal."

"But that's archaic! Nobody does that anymore. . . ."

"We're in prehistoric times, my boy."

"I'll get infected."

"Maybe not. They put hot stones into a leather bag full of water, and I washed the needle and that length of sinew she's using as thread. I made her wash her hands, too, but she seemed to know how. These people are probably cleaner than many so-called civilized people centuries later."

When the ivory needle went into his thigh, the pain seemed so terrible Jeff thought he couldn't stand it, but suddenly he could, because Yobo was pinching his earlobes to distract him and he remembered what one of his parents' friends had once told him.

Don't try to conquer pain. Accept it, go with it as the body's way of showing you it's in trouble. Reassure yourself and your body that the trouble is being taken care of and that you won't need the pain anymore.

54

The suturing was over so quickly that Jeff felt as if he were floating above his injury, watching with gratitude the way the old woman and Yobo gently bound his thigh with pieces of soft leather that held a fragrant, wet moss against the wound.

"They've soaked the moss in some kind of herbal solution," Yobo said. "I guess they know what they're doing. At any rate, what with all the various immunities built into us modern humans, your wound may not get infected."

"Is the old woman the chief of this tribe?"

"I think she is. When you were unconscious, she showed you to the rest of the tribe, always repeating the same two-syllable word. Wish I knew what it meant."

A young girl, her light hair in braids tied with beaded leather, knelt beside Jeff and offered him a drink that tasted terrible—but it was wet and he was thirsty. She smiled, showing perfect teeth, and gave him a drink from another bag. This seemed to be a tangy fruit juice that took away the horrible taste of what Jeff supposed was their idea of medicine.

Then he noticed a dark-haired woman, perhaps a few years older than himself, standing at the foot of his bed, staring at him. She'd apparently been crying, but now she looked angry. She made a sign with her hand, moving it from her heart to her forehead, and then—in a fist—toward Jeff.

The chief, as Jeff thought of the oldest, frowned at this woman, pointed to Jeff, and said the two-syllable word again.

The dark-haired woman shook her head no, made the same sign, and spat at Jeff.

Instantly the chief stood up, speaking angrily and raising her hand. The dark-haired woman burst into tears and ran into one of the smaller huts.

"What's all that about?" Jeff asked Yobo.

"I think the one who spat at you is the mother of that

child wounded by the mammoth. I also think the tribe believes I'm a magician who has transformed a female child into an adult male—you, Jeff. Except that the mother won't believe it."

The chief spoke to Yobo, pointing to the largest hut, a long rounded structure that was covered with hides.

"The sun is setting," Yobo said. "They want us to go inside. She had to operate out here while there was still daylight because they've only got stone lamps using animal fat and moss wicks."

As Yobo and another male pulled Jeff's bed into the large hut, Jeff saw that the arched doorway was made by two enormous mammoth tusks. A couple of pieces of hide had been pulled back to give light and air in the hut, probably because it was summer. For the same reason, there was no fire at the small hearth in the hut, only at the big fire pits outdoors.

Yobo sat down beside Jeff's bed and stroked the inside wall of the hut. Mammoth jaws and skulls were neatly stacked to make an interesting, interlocking pattern filled in with moss and dried mud. More curving tusks made the roof and held up the hides. Jeff was most surprised by the floor, for it was of carefully laid, rounded stones set into the dirt to make a dry surface that was then partly covered by thick pieces of leather. In its own way, the hut was beautiful, and the tribe had ornamented it with hanging panels of decorated leather. One panel had the picture of a mammoth burned into it.

"Quite a place, eh, Jeff? Wenoa Grachev once showed me the picture of a restored mammoth bone hut found in a place called Mezirich in the Soviet Union, as it was called then. This hut isn't the same, but it's similar."

"Maybe that's a picture of the mammoth that hurt me."

"Wouldn't be surprised," said Yobo, looking at the leather hanging. "Good artist. Too bad Rembrandt can't see this. Now, Jeff, I think you should try to sleep. . . ."

Jeff felt a little light-headed. "Silly old mammoth. It did seem like an old bull, Admiral, coming down to the river to drink, maybe with a tusk that was already cracked, and too big for the tribe to kill, or else they adopted it as a sort of mascot."

"After it tossed you into the river I saw the tribe chase it back, not with spears but by stomping on the ground and singing to beat the band. I suppose the tribe just kept out of its way when it brought the herd to drink, only the child was too young to understand. Now please, Jeff, try to sleep."

The young girl with fair hair entered the hut with a rush basket full of berries, roots, nuts, and charred meat. She offered it to Yobo, who started to give it to Jeff until the chief moved out of the shadows and pushed away his hand.

"Maybe this chief is also medicine woman for the tribe and has learned it's best to have a liquid diet after trauma, in case of internal injuries. I've examined you and I don't think you have any, but we'd best do as she wants. Good thing you ate on Rembrandt's ship. I wish Norby would come and take us to my ship."

"He'd be here if he could."

"Unfortunately he's a mixed-up robot who makes mistakes."

"I trust him," said Jeff. "He'll find us."

"I hope so." Yobo yawned and ate some food. "There's more boiled water in that bag near you. Drink as much as you can."

"But when I have to . . ."

"I'll carry you out. No problem."

"They'll all see."

Yobo laughed. "No point in being shy in this place." He methodically ate everything on the mat, although he made faces as he chewed through some of it.

In spite of his sleepiness, Jeff stayed awake and watched the twilight glow of deep sapphire in the sky through one of the openings in the bone and hide roof. Gradually the sky darkened and stars appeared, so Jeff knew that he was not in the far north, where the sun doesn't set completely all night in summer. He remembeerd that the ice-age glaciers covered much of North America but left a lot of Eurasia as open steppe, teeming with wildlife.

He heard some sad singing, as if the tribe were mourning the loss of a child, or perhaps the mysterious change of that child into an adult of the opposite sex, one who could not speak their language. He felt lost and sad, too, and in his physical weakness began to experience despair.

He told himself that despair wouldn't help. Instead, he tried thinking of a version of his solstice litany.

I am alive. I will try to relax and let my body heal. I will rejoice that I am a human being, part of Terran life on a beautiful living planet, in a solar system, in a galaxy, in a great big universe, and I will try to be worthy. . . .

He was asleep.

Danger in the Tribe

When morning came there were no clouds. Under a bright sun, the steppe was probably as warm as it ever got during the last ice age. Yobo propped the head of Jeff's bed upon a mammoth skull so he could sit up, looking out the tusk arch and across the central village compound to the rolling land beyond.

Jeff felt almost like a royal prince, for it seemed as if everyone in the tribe visited, bringing tidbits of food. Since all of the members of the tribe looked muscular and healthy, Jeff hoped the food would help make him the same, and besides he was hungry.

"I'm hungry enough to eat mammoth, which I suppose some of this meat is."

"The hunters brought in a deer and some rabbits this morning," Yobo said, studying a bone he had just been gnawing, "but I don't know what I'm eating. Try those eggs—not bad. I cooked them, I hope, in a hot-water bag. And we'll probably have fish later today—the youngsters are down by the river with bone fishhooks. Humanity hasn't changed much."

Jeff smiled and tried to enjoy the fact that he was reasonably safe and his wound hurt less, but he kept worrying about Norby. Was he alive?

"Your clothes are washed and hanging in the sun, Jeff. I hope you like the leather outfit you're wearing. The young girl who gave it to me giggled a lot. And speaking of attentive females, she's peeking around the door right now."

In a lordly manner, Jeff beckoned to the girl. When she

59

came in shyly, he pointed to himself and said, "Jeff." Then he pointed to her and raised his eyebrows.

She pointed to him and said "Jeff?" It was clearly a question, and when he nodded yes, she shook her head no. He decided he hadn't communicated adequately and tried again, but she kept shaking her head no. Finally she touched her own head and said something that sounded like "Mayla."

"Ah," said Yobo, pointing to her. "Mayla?"

She giggled, nodded yes, and ran out.

"Well, she doesn't like my name," Jeff said, "but I like hers and that's what I'll call her."

"Maybe it just means 'servant' or 'handmaiden' or whatever," said Yobo. "By the way, I notice that she's covered herself with jewelry this morning—ivory bracelets and anklets, and did you see the lump of amber hanging from that shell necklace? Amber and shells aren't found around here, so these people must trade with others."

"She's pretty," said Jeff, sighing a little.

"Watch out that she doesn't fall for you. She looks dolled up for a date, with stuff on those eyelashes of hers, presumably in order to bat them at you more effectively."

"Like the prime minister's eyelashes?"

"Cadet! That will do!"

"Yes, sir."

"Besides, after seeing Euterpe, no human woman can possibly measure up."

"Wouldn't you like to be the consort of this tribe's chief, who's still handsome—"

"Cadet! I have enough trouble with older women! Hey!"

"What's the matter, Admiral?"

"There's a woman hanging over your head. They must have put it there while we slept."

Jeff looked up and saw, hanging from the roof, a little ivory statuette in the shape of a voluptuously pregnant female.

60

Peering at it, Yobo said, "I'll have to learn the language of the tribe. Nobody's ever figured out exactly what those figurines were used for. Maybe she's hanging there to protect you, or to remind you that, once healed, you have masculine duties to perform. . . ."

"Admiral! I'm only fifteen!"

"Well into adulthood for them, I should imagine. I'd also like to ask the tribe about those perforated pieces of antler that our archaeologists call batons. Already this morning I've seen them used like multipurpose tools, as hammers and leather softeners and spear straighteners, but the chief has one that's decorated with carving and leather strips. I don't know what it's for, but I applaud the way these early humans make creative use of everything their environment offers, yet they don't try to control and dominate their world. They just live happily in it."

"You wanted hope, Admiral. Maybe these people find it in everyday life."

"I almost wish that Norby would never come back and we could stay, but winter's coming and then we'd be in real trouble. The only advantage of light skin is when you live in places where there isn't much sunlight in winter. Too much melanin prevents the absorption of ultraviolet rays and the manufacture of vitamin D."

"Since you can't take supplements, you'll have to eat lots of fish and the livers of animals, the way Eskimos—"

"Cadet, I am not an Eskimo, or fond of liver. I'll have to migrate south—and soon. This must be summer's end."

"As soon as my leg heals I'll go with you. If Norby comes back, he can tune in to my presence wherever I am."

"We may have to sneak away from the tribe, especially if they think I'm some sort of exotic god and you are the incarnation of one of their children. Blast it all, I wish I'd never bought that stupid holocamera, and had that idiotic notion of finding our ancestral elephant. It's my fault you're

61

wounded and we're stranded fifteen, twenty thousand years in the past."

"I wanted to come, Admiral. And Norby will find me. I have to go on believing that he's in the universe somewhere, some—*time*." Jeff swallowed and tried not to show that he was on the verge of tears. To distract Yobo, he pointed to a piece of bone propped up on the near wall. "While we wait, there's so much to study—I saw the chief come in this morning early and make a mark on that bone. There's a whole series of marks. It's probably a calendar. . . ."

Yobo's big hand squeezed Jeff's shoulder. "You're the bravest cadet I know."

This time the tears welled up, but didn't spill over because Mayla entered, arguing vociferously with a redheaded young man. With a defiant toss of her head, she sat down beside Jeff while the young man shook his fist at both.

"Admiral, is he her brother, urging me to marry her, or a former boyfriend angry because I might?"

"Interesting, Jeff. He has a bone spear thrower attached to his belt. It extends the force and range of any spear—"

"This is no time to be scientific, Admiral! I think he's not her brother."

"Mayla!" The chief was standing in the doorway.

Mayla rose at once and ran out without a glance at the young man, who followed her angrily. The chief sat down in the doorway, took out the broken tip of mammoth tusk, and proceeded to work on it.

"Amazing," said Yobo. "She's already split it in half and chosen this half to carve. It's the same half as my heirloom—see how it bends?"

"Admiral, I'm worried about Mayla's young man. Suppose he gets angry enough to dispose of me?"

"I think you should concentrate on Norby. We will both concentrate on him, bless his little domed hat and mixed-up insides."

"I thought his inefficiency annoyed you, Admiral."

"I'm trying to be charitable and think good thoughts to attract the little metal monster."

Norby did not come by nightfall, and Yobo carried Jeff out to the central campfire. As the moon had not yet risen, Jeff could marvel at the scintillating display of stars and planets in the clear sky.

"What's that!" Jeff exclaimed, for a light had flashed in the sky and the tribe made a strange chanting noise.

"For a moment I thought I was hallucinating a starship passing by," Yobo said, "but it's a meteor. This must be one of the regular showers of them. We don't have them on Mars, and the parts of Earth I've visited had such bright lights that I've never seen what people used to call shooting stars. I suppose this tribe believes that stars are actually falling out of the sky."

Jeff couldn't enjoy the meteor shower. He was uncomfortably aware of having two enemies. Near another hut, the redheaded boy glowered at him and talked to the dark-haired woman Yobo thought was the missing child's mother.

"I wonder if those two are conspiring to kill me."

"They probably won't do anything with me around," Yobo said, flexing his muscles, "and I'll always be around."

The rest of the tribe sat down near the campfire, now only glowing embers, not light enough to dim the sky view. The chief raised a piece of deer leg bone to her lips and Jeff saw that it had holes perforated in it. As she blew into one end an eerie wailing sound issued from the instrument.

"It's a concert!" whispered Yobo, touching Euterpe's music recording device, still on the tunic he was wearing over his paleolithic leather clothes. "I hope this is recording."

An old man began to use antler hammers upon a drum of mammoth skull decorated in bright colors, perhaps from berry and leaf juices. The sound was deep and resonant, in a rhythm that wound in and with the playing of the chief. Next to him another man began to drum softly on a big, hollow mammoth thigh bone—"the way my African ancestors drummed on hollow tree trunks," Yobo said. "People are like other people."

An older woman tapped short dry sticks together and another blew through a small bone that whistled. As the various instruments synchronized, the rest of the tribe joined in by chanting, as if they were paying homage to the close of day and beginning of night. Soon it was a melody that soared in wildness every time another meteor fell.

Time passed, and then Jeff saw a glow on the horizon. The full moon rose beyond the undulations of the steppe, and the chief stood up. She put down her wind instrument and took up the baton Yobo had seen.

Down the length of the baton was a simple curved design, and through the hole were threaded several thin, brightly colored strips of leather, each with a bead sewn at the tip. The strips fluttered from the baton like long hairs, and as the chief swung the baton over her head, back and forth, it made a swishing, rattling noise while she sang.

"A wand, Jeff. Magic. She's singing and signaling to the moon."

The strange music was so moving that Jeff wanted to tell them to sing and play forever so he could forget that he was wounded and lost in a time not his own, but suddenly it stopped. The chief sat down by the fire and began working on the tusk point.

At once the redheaded young man leapt to his feet and brandished a short daggerlike spear toward Jeff while the rest of the tribe murmured and moved back into the shadows. The chief ignored everything but her carving.

"Interesting," said Yobo. "Many male animals have ritual combat to decide the choice of mates, and humans seem to be no exception. Look how Mayla is simpering about it."

"How can I fight him when I'm laid up?"

"You have a proxy, Jeff. Me."

"Admiral! You can't—I'm only a cadet—it isn't right, and

64

besides, you don't have a weapon and nobody's giving you one and he's younger than you are—"

"Bah," Yobo said, springing to his feet in one motion, something Jeff had not thought possible for the majestic figure of Space Command's chief admiral. Yobo moved his right foot forward, his legs slightly apart and his knees bent.

"Please, Admiral . . ."

"Shut up, Jeff. I've just remembered the word they used for proxy, someone who fights in the place of someone else."

"What is it?"

"Champion." With that, Yobo watched as the young man advanced, holding the short spear up in one fist. Yobo smiled. It was not a nice smile.

With a loud yell, the redhead leapt at Yobo, who bent to one side and crashed the edge of his hand against the boy's wrist. The spear fell, but the boy wheeled and leapt at Yobo again, hands outstretched.

Yobo leaned back, encouraging the boy's advance, but when the hands were almost at his throat Yobo roared. His own hands moved fast and the redhead seemed to fly over Yobo's shoulder into the campfire.

Calmly, the admiral plucked the boy out of the fire, emptied Jeff's drinking bag over the sparks in his hair, and patted him on the shoulder. The boy groveled at Yobo's feet.

"Get up, blast you," muttered the admiral. "I'm out of practice. Didn't mean to throw you that far." To the redhead, it must have sounded as if Yobo were growling, for he moaned and bent lower.

Yobo stalked away, picked up Mayla, and dumped her near the redhead. The girl clung to the boy, Yobo pointed to one of the huts, and the two ran there, passing the horrified white face of the dark-haired woman.

There was absolute silence in the tribe until Yobo laughed, and then the tribe laughed, all but the child's mother, who sat down, crying.

"You didn't kill him, the way he would have killed me," Jeff said. "They're relieved. And I'm so grateful."

Yobo picked Jeff up and carried him to the long hut. "Time for sleeping."

One of the older men entered and handed Jeff two long sticks that were forked at one end. "Crutches! They've made crutches for me!"

"Easier to get away," Yobo said as the man went out. "I'm somewhat bushed, but don't worry—I'll wake if you call me. Good night, Jeff."

Soon Yobo was asleep—the sleep of the just, thought Jeff. But I have to find Norby.

He heard a faint noise and saw that the chief was sitting in the doorway, blocking the way in—or the way out. She clutched the ivory tusk, now carved on both sides, but not on the bottom, and occasionally murmured something, holding the ivory toward Jeff and Yobo as if warding off their evil.

We are evil, thought Jeff, if they have to live their lives contaminated by two strangers from the future.

Jeff closed his eyes, trying to shut out the prickles of pain from his healing wound, and called to Norby in his mind.

Norby, wherever and whenever you are, please tune in to me. I need you. Admiral Yobo needs you. This is not our time and place, although it is full of good things like an uncrowded world, clear skies, and beautiful music. I want to go home, Norby. Please come!

Jeff's thoughts seemed to spread out from his mind as if he were shaking them at the universe the way the chief had shaken her "wand" at the moon, whose light at this moment outlined the seated form of the woman in the doorway.

Jeff went to sleep, but not for long. The moonlight and the chief were stil there when a telepathic voice woke him.

—Jeff, I've been having a terrible time finding you. Couldn't you have concentrated on me?

10.

Disappearance

Jeff grabbed Norby and hugged him. He also made telepathic contact. —Norby, get us out of here!

—The admiral's asleep, Jeff, but that woman sitting in the doorway is awake. Why isn't she yelling? Why is she holding up the admiral's heirloom—isn't it back in the ship?

—I don't know the answers to any of those questions, but I suspect she thinks we're evil, especially now you've arrived. I'll wake up the admiral and we must leave at once. Since you can't take us both through hyperspace, we'll go outside and you can antigrav us back to the ship.

—There's a little problem. . . .

—You can't antigrav?

—Sure I can, but I think I ought to tell you . . .

—Norby, she's beginning to chant, and if the rest of the tribe comes, we'll have trouble getting away. I'm injured and the admiral will have to carry me, and you pick up him.

—Jeff! I go away for a few minutes and you get injured!

—That was day before yesterday, this time.

—Jeff leaned over and tapped Yobo, who woke instantly. Finger at his lips, Yobo smiled at Norby and quickly handed Jeff his old clothes and crutches.

"I don't think the loss of the tunics and leggings we're wearing will harm the tribe," Yobo said softly. "And you'd better take your crutches with you just in case you need them before we get back to civilization." He lifted Jeff and started for the doorway.

The chief rose, blocking the exit, and Yobo stopped.

"I don't want to hurt her, but I will if I must."

"Norby," said Jeff, "maybe she'll move out of the way if *you* walk toward her. I just hope she doesn't scream."

Norby's legs shot out of his metal body. He lowered his head until it was hard to see his eyes under the shadow of his domed hat. He marched very deliberately right at the chief.

Jeff couldn't help thinking that an animated barrel with a lid on it was a humorous sight, but Norby must have looked monstrous to the chief, for she paled and ran to a patch of moonlight outside the hut.

"Out we go," said Yobo, following Norby.

"Stand right there, Admiral," said Norby. "Hold Jeff tightly and I'll lift you. I sense that the *Pride* is still fixed on its antigrav over this area, safe and sound. We'd better hurry before the chief decides to scream and wakes everyone up."

The chief did not scream, not even when Norby lifted Yobo and Jeff off the ground. Jeff looked down and saw her staring upward at them, until they were so high up they couldn't see her any more in the moonlight.

The ship had never seemed so modern, so comfortable, and so safe before. It cleaned and repaired Jeff's clothes, and provided a regulated atmosphere and running water as well as toilets, towels, soap, and sanitary bandages for his wound.

"I don't seem to have stocked the ship with a woundseal," Yobo said sadly. "You'd better be careful not to strain that wound. There's only one suture and it's not exactly modern."

Jeff had finished explaining everything to Norby while he put his own clothes back on. "That's our story, Norby. Now please tell us what happened to you and why you were late."

"I'm so sorry, Jeff."

"It's all right, Norby. You couldn't have stopped the mammoth from goring me, and now that it's over I'm glad I had two days on ice-age Earth. But what happened to you? Did you take the child to Rembrandt?"

"Yes. She's still there, and—"

Yobo interrupted. "Since we should see about the child, it might as well be Rembrandt who tends Jeff's wound. Maybe he'll have something better than the woundheal I can get at Space Command hospital. Let's go now, Norby."

"I don't think we should, Admiral."

"And just why not?"

"I think history's already been changed."

"Because we went to paleolithic Earth!"

"I think so. History had already been changed before I arrived at Rembrandt's ship, because when I got there, it was awful. I barely got away. . . ."

"Norby!" Jeff shouted. "What are you talking about!"

"I arrived from hyperspace into the middle of that observation lounge of his. He was there, and I explained that we'd been responsible for the child getting hurt by the mammoth, or else responsible for the child not getting killed by the mammoth. . . ."

Yobo groaned. "We don't know which one of those is the problem. We don't know whether or not to take the child back."

"Or maybe it's not the child at all," Jeff said slowly, feeling scared inside. "Maybe the admiral and I did something while we were trapped with the tribe. Something that changed history—but Norby, you haven't explained how history has been changed!"

"I'm getting there, if you two wouldn't interrupt. Rembrandt said he would try to cure the child if he could, but when I thanked him in Terran Basic, by mistake, he looked as if he couldn't understand me. Then two strong machines like boxes with arms came into the room and grabbed me. I asked Rembrandt why and he said I was obviously a time traveler of some sort."

"But he knows you can time-travel!" said Jeff.

"That's just it, Jeff. Rembrandt didn't know me at all! He said I had to be taken to a tribunal of the Others because they don't approve of time travel and they had to find out who I am and if I'm dangerous."

"I don't understand," said Yobo. "And how did you get away from Rembrandt's ship?"

"I surprised the robot guards by drawing in my arms and legs, and then I went into hyperspace, where they couldn't follow. Either Rembrandt has lost his memory, or history's changed. Do you realize what that means?"

Yobo massaged his skull. "One way or the other, Rembrandt doesn't remember you, or any of us, since you told him about us getting into problems on ice-age Earth. It's possible that in this new time track, human civilization never progressed to space travel, except that we're here, in a spaceship, aren't we? I certainly feel 'here.'"

"Since I took your ship into hyperspace," Norby said, "and I made it possible for all of us to meet Rembrandt, it's much more likely that in this time track human civilization hasn't progressed to *me!*"

Jeff couldn't laugh. "We must find out what we did to put history on a different track."

"I suppose we should first find out more about the false track," Yobo said. "Perhaps nothing's wrong except Rembrandt."

Jeff and Norby looked at each other, and Norby said, "If that's the case, maybe we changed Rembrandt's ancestors, since a few of them visited ice-age Earth to pick up specimens of animals and humans. That's how they colonized the planet Izz.* If our visit to the paleolithic tribe did something to make them so afraid of strangers that later they kill Rembrandt's ancestors . . ."

"No, Norby," said Jeff. "Izz is populated by humans taken

*See *Norby and the Lost Princess.*

from every part of Earth, so what we did to one little tribe wouldn't change the subsequent history of the Others."

"It would if they killed an important ancestor of Rembrandt," said Yobo.

"But Rembrandt still exists!" said Jeff. "Did he look the same to you, Norby?"

"Exactly the same. Perhaps it means that you and I don't exist in the new time track, Jeff. We're the ones who found Rembrandt and made friends with him."

Yobo thumped on the control panel. "See here, all this speculation is getting us nowhere, and we have to go somewhere. I propose going to this false Rembrandt's ship and seeing what's what. He's in hyperspace, but it's up in our own time, and not only do I want to find out what's going on there, but Jeff's leg needs attention."

"And we can't just leave a human child with the Others," Jeff said. "We must go, Norby."

As Norby plugged himself into the ship's computer once more, Jeff looked at ice-age Earth in the viewscreen. He knew now that it was populated by humans called primitive by people of his own time, but who had their own way of living life—with art, music, and justice.

Earth winked out, replaced by the gray of hyperspace.

"I had a lot of trouble time traveling when I left Rembrandt's ship in hyperspace," Norby said. "That's why I was late getting back to you. And why I'm having trouble now."

"You mean that we're in hyperspace but you haven't moved the ship forward in time?" asked Yobo.

"Right," said Norby.

"Maybe it's because you're trying to get to Rembrandt and he's wrong. Take us directly to Space Command, our time, and we'll have my doctors fix Jeff's wound."

"Okay, sir," said Norby, shutting his back eyes to concentrate. "I'm trying again. It's very hard, but I think—yes, we're in our own time now. I'm sure of it."

"But we're still in hyperspace," said Jeff. "Take us into normal space."

"I can't, Jeff. There's nothing wrong with the ship but I just can't get out of hyperspace." Norby opened his back eyes.

"Jeff! The admiral's gone!"

11.

Finding Out

Jeff and Norby searched the *Pride* but the answer was the same. Admiral Yobo was gone.

"I'm sorry, Jeff. Whatever changed history, it means that the admiral isn't in the ship with us now, in our own time. It's probable that he's in Space Command, but if I can get the ship out of hyperspace and we go to see him, he won't know us any more than Rembrandt knew me."

"Because we don't exist in what used to be our own time," said Jeff. "That must be it, Norby. And that's why you *can't* take the ship out of hyperspace."

"Time paradoxes upset my cognitive circuits, Jeff."

"And my head aches. I have a heartache, too, because of the admiral's disappearance." Jeff fought back panic. Never before had he realized how much he missed a father. He'd had a brother ten years older as a substitute, but nobody had filled the role better than Boris Yobo.

"Jeff, I think we'd better try going back slowly in time until we do find a moment when I can get us out of hyperspace."

"Do it, Norby. There must be a way we can find out what happened so we can go back and correct it."

The control room was silent while Norby concentrated on time travel, then suddenly he said, "This is it! The first chance we have to get out of hyperspace into normal space. I think it's not too far back, either—maybe around sixteen years or so."

"Jut before I was born. Maybe that's the reason you can go into normal space now. Let's go to Space Command—if

73

it's only sixteen years in the past, Yobo will be there, not as chief admiral, but that doesn't matter. He won't know us, but maybe he'll let you use a records computer to find out things, and surely he'll help me get to a regular doctor."

"Well—here goes." Norby gripped the control switches and the viewscreen changed.

"You missed Space Command, Norby. You've brought the ship right to the Yobo airlock on Mars."

"Perhaps I just overshot the mark, or"—Norby blinked rapidly—"perhaps some of my circuits decided to come here first. I'm not doing too well, Jeff."

"You're doing the best you can, under difficult circumstances. Now that we're here, maybe it's better to visit the admiral's sister and speak to Yobo on hycom. We can ask him about the Federation and my family without revealing that you can time-travel."

"We? How can you go down to the house? You can't walk."

"I'll manage on the crutches."

Going down in the elevator was easy, and this time Jeff hobbled into the little car that met them at the pavilion.

"This is reassuring," Jeff said. "Even if this is sixteen years ago, the house looks just the same."

"The garden's a little different."

"Because it's spring. The garden's all flowering bulbs and fruit trees right now."

When Jeff extricated himself from the little car, he wished he'd thought to have Norby carry him, for there was a sudden pain in his leg. He didn't have time to worry about it, however, because the front door of the Yobo mansion opened and an old-fashioned robot butler stood there.

"Welcome, sirs. Your names?"

"Jeff Wells, and this is my robot, Norby."

"Please state your reason for coming to the Yobo mansion."

"To visit Mrs. Yobo."

74

"There is no Mrs. Yobo, sir. Prime Minister Yobo resides here but is now in Federation Spome, presiding over Federation Parliament."

"Prime minister! What does he look like?"

"The way he always has, sir. Would you like to see his latest holoportrait?"

"Yes, please."

"Come this way." The butler showed them into the hall, but Norby had to help Jeff by turning on his antigrav just enough to glide them both over the marble floor.

When they entered the Yobo living room, there was a large portrait of a man in full Federation regalia, the kind a prime minister wears during opening ceremonies of Parliament.

"He looks a little like the Yobo we know," said Jeff, "but he's not the same."

"This is Prime Minister Kinta Yobo, sir."

"A relative of Admiral Boris Yobo?"

There was a short pause while the robot butler stared straight ahead. Then it said, "I have a full history of the Yobo family in my memory banks, sir. There is no record of a Boris Yobo."

"Is there an Elizabeth Victoria Yobo?"

"No, sir."

—Jeff [Norby said telepathically], we must find out about your family, and the Grachevs.

—I think we're wearing out our welcome, Norby. I saw a big guard robot waiting in the hall outside.

"Robot," Norby said in his most authoritarian voice, "does this mansion have access to Computer Prime—the solar system still has Computer Prime, doesn't it? Keeping all the records on everybody and everything?"

"You speak strangely," said the butler. "I am not required to answer the questions of another robot."

"Answer it," Jeff said firmly.

"Yes, sir, there is an outlet in this room, but you may not use it without presenting proper identification as one of the

75

prime minister's staff. Mere tourists are requested to walk through the mansion and touch nothing."

"I must reach Computer Prime!" Norby exclaimed.

"I am sorry, sir, but your robot is illogical and poorly programmed. I am requesting security forces to deal with you."

A large robot stomped into the room, while another stood at the doorway.

Jeff deliberately slid one crutch out from under him so that he fell on his good leg. It was hard on the bad leg, for over the wound on his thigh the cloth suddenly felt warm and wet. He was bleeding again.

"Mr. Butler, I am wounded and cannot stand up for long. Please let me rest on that couch over there for a few minutes. You see, I know the prime minister, who was—I mean will be—I mean . . ." Jeff's voice trailed off. He hated to lie.

"The prime minister was delighted to meet Jeff," Norby said truthfully, although the truth applied to a different time track, "and will not be pleased that you endangered my master's health." Without waiting for consent, Norby picked Jeff up and took him to the couch.

—This robot isn't very intelligent [said Norby].

—The guard doesn't look smart, either, but they're both bigger than we are.

"I have notified the humans in charge of the mansion," said the butler. "When they come, they will decide what to do with you."

—I know where the outlet to Computer Prime is, Jeff. Exactly where it is in our Yobo's living room.

—I've gotten us fixed in this room, Norby, but I don't see how you're going to use the outlet with the butler and the guard watching us.

—I could go into hyperspace and come out smack on their heads, one by one. Then as soon as they're disabled . . .

—You can't do that! It isn't right!

76

—These robots don't really exist, any more than Kinte Yobo does. It's a false time track.

—But we're in it, and they exist here. I'm probably responsible for the loss of the true time track and I don't want anything else damaged.

—You always take too much guilt on yourself, Jeff. I think I know who's responsible for the mess we're in. But first I have to make certain, and I have to use Computer Prime. I can't if these blasted robots stop me.

—That's the answer, Norby! A robot has the right to protect its own existence.

—You mean that by the laws of robotics it's all right for these blasted behemoths to scobble me instead of me scobbling them?

—No, no! I mean that don't you have to recharge now and then? And if you can't do it in hyperspace, you can use ordinary electricity, can't you?

—Jeff, you're a genius, too!

Norby began to walk around the room, lurching from side to side and blinking his eyes erratically. He made squeaking noises and seemed to be grinding mysterious gears every time he passed the Computer Prime outlet.

"What is the matter with your robot, sir?" asked the butler. "He should be destroyed if he functions so poorly."

At that, Norby's head sank into his body until only the tops of his eyes showed. The big guard robot moved toward him.

Jeff held up his hand. "Wait. My robot often needs recharging. He functions perfectly when charged up. If you do not permit him to recharge, I will report to the prime minister that you are guilty of causing the deactivation of my personal, and very expensive, property."

The guard and the butler looked at each other. Then their heads turned toward Jeff, and back to look at Norby.

"Recharging is of course a necessity for all robots," the butler said slowly.

Norby's barrel closed up and slowly rolled across the floor to rest against the wall, directly under the outlet to Computer Prime.

"That is not the recharging outlet," said the butler.

"My robot knows where to recharge," said Jeff. "I insist that you leave him alone while he is plugged in."

Norby's sensor wire snaked out from the knob on his hat and plugged into the outlet to Computer Prime.

"But . . ." the butler said.

"Obey me, robot," Jeff said at the top of his lungs. "My robot needs to use that outlet!"

Suddenly Jeff heard voices coming closer, and some of them were human voices. "Norby! Hurry!"

Norby's sensor wire withdrew. His barrel elevated and shot over to Jeff, head, arms, and legs emerging on the way.

"The window, Norby!" Holding his crutches, Jeff let Norby pick him up and fly through the open window to the garden just as two more robots and three humans burst into the Yobo living room.

Before the guards could catch up, Norby made it through the two airlocks and into the *Pride* control room, depositing Jeff gently upon the floor before he rushed to plug himself in and make the safety of hyperspace close around them.

"What did you find out from Computer Prime, Norby?"

"The Wells family is intact."

"That's good, but . . ."

"Jeff, there are also some Yobos and Grachevs, but not our admiral or our prime minister. Remember that in the correct time track, it was Admiral Yobo who gave you the money and the order to buy a teaching robot. You and I will never meet in this time track!"

12.

Finding

Inside *The Pride of Mars*, Jeff examined his freshly bleeding wound. To his dismay, he discovered that the primitive suture had come apart. He put on a tight pressure bandage, but the wound hurt and he was afraid it was getting infected.

"What do we do now, Jeff?"

"First tell what you meant when you said you knew who was responsible for the change of time tracks. Yobo and I?"

"Not exactly. I mean that's not my theory. But if I check my theory, history might be changed *again*, and for the worse. In this time track your family exists and eventually you will."

"I want Admiral Yobo to exist! And sixteen years from now, where you and I can't go in this time track, there's a Jeff Wells who won't have a robot named Norby. I don't care what your theory is, Norby. Just check it out so we can get back our own time track and go home."

Norby went to the control board. "I don't want to plug in. I'm upset about my theory. I can't be certain. . . ."

"Certainty is hard to come by in any universe, Norby."

"We have to go to dangerous places. . . ."

"You are talking to someone who's gone to ice-age Earth in clothes suitable for tropical Africa, been gored by a mammoth, thrown into a cold river, sutured with animal sinew by a blunt ivory needle in the hands of a medicine woman who's been dead at least fifteen thousand years. . . ."

"But Jeff . . ."

"Furthermore, I've drunk horrible medicine, eaten primitive food, slept on smelly hides, and been fought over by a paleolithic girl's jealous boyfriend. I should have been protecting my admiral, but instead it was he who saved my life, and now he's disappeared into nonexistence. Will you please tell me your theory and what we have to do about it?"

There was a small silence, while Norby blinked. "Your story is very sad, and there's a villain in it."

"Who?"

"Me."

Norby managed to look so pathetic that in spite of his anxiety Jeff almost laughed out loud. "Norby, old friend, don't tell me any more. Letting out all my complaints helped clear my brain, so give me another chance to reason out what made the time track change."

Norby jiggled on his feet and hummed, out of tune as usual, while Jeff took a deep breath and thought hard.

"Of course. You took the paleolithic child to Rembrandt's ship, and she's still there. When we entered that time period, Yobo disappeared, so it must be because the child was removed from history."

"By me, Jeff. History changed as soon as I took her away from her own time, so that when I brought her to Rembrandt's ship it was already wrong. Rembrandt had never met me before."

"That's right, Norby. We assumed that the little girl was injured only because we entered the past. That may or may not be true, because she might have been hurt by the mammoth anyway, but the point is that she's supposed to survive and live with her tribe, marry, and have children. . . ."

"Some of whom became the ancestors of the Grachevs. That means that Wenoa Grachev's great-great-granduncle must have been *very* good friends with Admiral Yobo's great-great-grandmother—otherwise we'd still have our admiral."

"We must get the child away from Rembrandt's ship and take her back to the tribe so her genes can enter history."

Robot and master stared at each other unhappily.

80

"Jeff, what if Rembrandt holds us in custody for that time-travel tribunal or whatever it is?"

"If we're caught, we'll have to talk our way out of the tribunal. But let's try not to get caught. We must steal the child—and don't waggle a finger at me, Norby. Remember that we're only trying to undo the previous stealing of the child away from the tribe."

"You stay here in the ship, Jeff. I'll hyperjump directly to Rembrandt's ship and take the child."

"I don't like that. The Others are so much more advanced than we are. Suppose Rembrandt has ways of preventing you from leaving that he hasn't used yet? Besides, you can't prove the child should go with you, and I can, because the little girl and I are both human. She should be with her own kind, not with the Others."

"It isn't safe. I'm going alone. . . ."

Jeff was struggling into his leather tunic and leggings. "Norby, if you disappear into time without me, I will never speak to you again. And if something happened so that you couldn't come back to the ship, I'd be stuck here in hyper-space because only you can take the ship out of it. I'd be alone—and forever."

"All right, Jeff. Don't you think I ought to join the *Pride*'s airlock to that of Rembrandt's ship? We could just walk inside and . . ."

"And into a tribunal? No, thanks. We'll leave the ship here, back sixteen years and in hyperspace. Then you take me directly from this control room to the observation room on Rembrandt's ship, sixteen years ahead. If the Others chase us, we can escape because they can't time-travel."

Norby put his extendable arms around Jeff's chest. "I'm ready, Jeff. Scared, but ready."

"Then let's go. Try to be accurate!"

Jeff felt the shivery sensation of being in the nothingness of hyperspace, and then he was back in the majestic observation lounge of Rembrandt's ship, gazing at a female Other singing to a sleepy human child.

"Euterpe!" Jeff exclaimed before he could stop himself.

The child whimpered and squirmed off the Other's lap to the floor, gazing wide-eyed at the spectacle of a human boy hanging in air from the arms of a silvery barrel with half a head, lidded eyes, and a domed hat.

"Who are you and why do you say that strange word?" asked Euterpe, in the language of the Others.

Jeff used the same language and said, "I am the child's relative." It was truthful enough. "I have come to take her home. She needs medical help."

Euterpe's lower arms wrapped around the child's body, and one of her upper arms caressed the curly brown hair. "Your body's configuration is similar to that of the child, but you must prove that you are her relative. She does not seem to recognize you. I have cured her and she is mine, now."

—Jeff, how are you going to get the child away from her before Rembrandt and the posse show up?"

—Shut up, Norby. Let me think.

"And how did you get inside our ship?" asked Euterpe. "You and your robot are strange, and probably dangerous. . . ."

"I assure you that I mean no harm to your ship, and that I am sincerely grateful that you have cured the child. I am her distant relative, the only one capable of traveling to your ship in order to bring her back to her people."

"We Others have determined that she is from the past, so you two are time travelers. We disapprove of time travel, so you must be investigated." Euterpe gestured to the wall. "I have sent for my brother. I am sure the tribunal will decide that you and this child have forfeited the right to return to the past. The child is *mine* now!"

—Females in all species are stubborn, Jeff. Have you noticed that?

—All I know is that she's a beautiful, compelling person and I'm having a hard time thinking.

—She's bewitching you somehow.

—No, I just feel sorry for her.

—You'll have to explain to these Others that this is a wrong time track, and that there's another Rembrandt who knows us in the right time track. . . .

—Knows us—knows—that's it, Norby!

"I know this child, ma'am, even if she does not know me. I can prove it." Jeff had suddenly recaptured the two-syllable word used by the members of the tribe when pointing to Jeff, the word that caused the child's mother to shake her head no.

Jeff said the word as clearly as he could, smiled, and beckoned to the little girl.

With a happy cry, she tore herself out of Euterpe's many arms and ran toward Jeff just as Rembrandt entered the room.

Jeff scooped up the child, held her tightly to him, and said in Terran Basic, "To the paleolithic, Norby."

They blinked in and out of hyperspace so fast that Jeff felt his stomach had been left behind, but whatever Norby had done, it was incredibly accurate, for the scene was exactly the same as the moment they'd left the chief staring up at them as they flew to the ship.

Not quite the same, for this time the chief was holding her face in her hands, and she was crying. The ivory tusk point was lying on the ground beside her as if abandoned because it was useless.

The chief looked up as Norby deposited Jeff and the child on the ground just in front of her.

Saying the two-syllable word, Jeff released the child, who ran crowing with delight to the strong arms of the chief.

The old woman also said the word, over and over, laughing and nuzzling the face of the child.

"That was her name, wasn't it?" asked Norby.

"Yes. Time to go."

Norby picked up Jeff again and rose into the air, but the chief, holding the child with one hand, called to them.

"I don't know what she's saying," said Jeff. "Could it be a thank-you?"

"We have to go, Jeff."

"Wait—she's picking up the heirloom."

The chief smiled up at Jeff and held the piece of ivory out toward him. She spoke again, pleadingly.

"She wants you to have it," said Norby. "I suppose that it's her gift to us because we brought back the child and the chief realizes that you aren't the little girl transformed after all. She must have thought so to begin with because they couldn't find the child and there you were, with very much the same curly brown hair."

"I can't take the gift."

"Why not? We found out its true history, and for all we know, it's not going to be in the ship's safe anymore. We may need this tusk to take back to our own time."

"We can't, Norby. It isn't finished yet. See—she's holding the blunt end out to us, and there's nothing carved on it. The heirloom still has to go through history."

"Wave good-bye, Jeff."

The grayness of hyperspace closed around Jeff again, and he cried a little himself. He thought that he would never forget the sight of the chief's face, full of hope and joy as he gave her back the lost child. He imagined the chief taking the child to the mother, and how the tribe would sing that night, in gratitude.

—Norby, I'll miss that ancient world of the paleolithic.

—I won't. I'm having trouble getting back to our own time. All this bouncing around on different time tracks has unsettled my circuits.

—Concentrate, Norby! We have to find the ship. The air in your protective field won't last forever, especially here in hyperspace.

—Tune in, Jeff. I need help.

Jeff felt Norby's grip on him tighten, and he tried to focus his own mind.

The Pride of Mars. Jeff tried to see its control room in his mind, all the while conscious of the fact that his leg hurt and that blood was seeping through all the new bandages and the leather legging.

Suddenly they seemed to burst into the universe of normal space-time, and Jeff landed with a thud on the control-room floor. He groaned with pain.

"Hey, Jeff, how did you get back into that outfit?" said a familiar bass voice. "And why?"

"Oh, Admiral! I'm so glad to see you!"

Yobo was seated in the control chair, looking just as resplendent as always in the uniform he had donned after leaving the ice age. "Have I missed something?"

Jeff stifled an impulse to run over and hug the admiral. Besides, he couldn't even walk at the moment. "Norby and I fixed things, sir, but I'd like Rembrandt to heal my leg."

"But Rembrandt won't know us—what do you mean, fixed things? When did you do that?"

"We restored the past," Norby said, waving a hand negligently as if it were all in a day's work.

"But when—and where was I?"

That was the difficult question to answer, thought Jeff. How do you tell a proud man like Boris Yobo that in one of the possible time tracks of the universe, he couldn't exist because a certain pale paleolithic child was taken from her own time?

"It's very simple," Norby said before Jeff could touch him and communicate telepathically the need to be tactful. "Your family DNA has genes in it from all the way back to that paleolithic tribe, thanks to your playful African great-great-grandmother and her affair with that Russian cosmonaut, so until we restored the missing child to her family, you didn't exist in the future. I mean, in our present. The one we belong in, that is. The false time track . . ."

"Left me out," said Yobo, stroking his big chin.

"Just a few genes, Admiral." Jeff paused. "I mean, presumably all your other ancestors were as your sister thinks they were, before and after the, uh . . ."

"I think, cadet, that I had better hear the whole story."

Jeff and Norby explained, winding up with the poignant picture of the chief clasping Yobo's remote little ancestor in her arms.

"Touching," Yobo said, dabbing at one eye. "Very. And you risked your lives and reopened your wound just to put me back into existence."

"Yes, sir."

"Thank you," Yobo said gravely.

"You're not annoyed at what we've discovered about your family tree, Admiral?" asked Norby.

The muscles in Yobo's face twitched. "Annoyed?" He threw his head back with a mighty laugh. "Good old great-great-grandmother!"

His laughter was so catching that Jeff began to chuckle and soon the two humans were laughing uproariously.

"Jeff. Admiral!" Norby waited, and when they didn't pay attention to him, he banged his metal fist on the control board.

"What is it, Norby?" Yobo said, wiping his eyes. "Oh, of course. We must attend to Jeff's wound. Take us right to Rembrandt—the right Rembrandt, of course."

Norby plugged in. "By the way, Admiral, while we're getting Jeff cured, don't you think you'd better figure out some way of explaining your heritage to your sister?"

Yobo clapped his hand to his forehead and rolled his eyes upward.

13.

The Secret of the Carving

"Go ahead, Jeff. Try walking around the room."

Jeff looked at Rembrandt doubtfully but stood up anyway and tried a few tentative steps. There was no pain, no blood running down his leg, and his thigh felt only slightly stiff.

"Amazing," he said. "I'm so grateful to you, Rembrandt. How did you get the wound to heal so quickly after I broke it open again?"

"A combination of electrotherapy and a topical medicine that's an improvement on the woundseal your Federation uses."

Yobo nodded. "I'd give anything to have the formula."

Rembrandt smiled. He touched one of Yib's outlets and shut all three of his eyes as if he were communing with his ship's computer. In a few seconds, a plasti-card dropped from a slit and Rembrandt handed it to Yobo.

"The formula is yours, Admiral. Tell your research people that it was given to you by an old witch doctor."

"Ah, yes," said Yobo, with a grin. "They'll think it was handed down by my African ancestors." Then the corners of his mouth turned down, and his whole face seemed to droop. "I just can't imagine how I'm going to break the news to my sister that our ancestry is much more mixed up than she thinks it is."

"Sisters can certainly make brothers apprehensive," said Rembrandt solemnly.

"You too?"

"Absolutely, Admiral. At this very moment I am apprehensive about my sister's state of mind. You see, if I don't take you to her, not just to say good-bye but to talk awhile, she will be, shall we say, disapproving?''

''You mean she'll blame you if Jeff and Norby and I leave immediately?''

''I am afraid so.''

''There's no problem, Rembrandt.'' Yobo smoothed down his Space Command uniform, which looked considerably better than the torn cotton tunic he'd discarded in the *Pride*. ''I want very much to see your sister again. Saying good-bye is the hard part. She is a strangely compelling female.''

'' 'Strangely compelling' is, I believe, the phrase I would also choose,'' said Rembrandt. ''Perhaps we should go to her at once, while she is still in a good mood.''

''Jeff, where's Norby?'' asked Yobo.

''I don't know. He came to the clinic room with us but he must have left. Sometimes biological things bother him, especially when I'm hurt.''

''Then we must find him—and see my sister.''

As Rembrandt led the way back to the observation lounge, Jeff thought that he would never have been able to find it himself, for the Others' ship was immense, with complicated corridors cued in special colors almost too subtle for a human to recognize. The artificial gravity was also much better than anything the Federation ships could achieve.

Yobo and Jeff had not yet told Rembrandt the full story of their adventures. They were worried about how he would react to knowing about the second Rembrandt, who lived in the false time track and didn't know his former friends.

In the observation lounge, Norby was standing near Euterpe, who looked as upset as an Other can manage.

''Norby,'' Jeff said, ''you've told her!''

''No, I haven't!''

''What is the matter, sister?'' asked Rembrandt.

''I am a musician, brother. My mind, my emotions, and my working career are dedicated to *music*—''

''I know, dear sister. You are the best.''

"—and fond as I am of your friends, and of this cute little robot, I would ask one favor."

"Anything, dear lady," said Yobo, drawn to the seat by her side as if she were a powerful electromagnet attuned to the iron in his red blood corpuscles.

"Please don't let Norby sing to me anymore."

"I was only singing our favorite Space Academy songs," Norby said. "When you tried to interrupt me, Euterpe, I thought it was just that you couldn't hear well, so I sang a little louder."

"Norby," Jeff said sternly, "you never admit that you sing off-key. Perhaps anyone who sings off-key doesn't know that he does, but you do and it must be painful to a marvelous musician like Euterpe."

She seemed to be suppressing a shudder. "I must go and listen to some genuine music that will make me feel better."

"Don't go, Euterpe," Yobo said, handing her the recording device that had been fixed to his African tunic. "The music captured by your device may not please your auditory organs, but perhaps you will find it interesting."

At Euterpe's gesture, a pedestal rose from the floor. She put the recording device on it and touched a gold spot at the edge. "Is this the music of your ancestors, Admiral?"

"Well, yes. I suppose it is."

Music filled the alien room and Jeff was once more back in the glow of the fire embers, watching shooting stars as a primitive orchestra made music that was as young as that planet seemed to be. Shutting his eyes, he could almost see the chief as she blew through the bone flute.

When the music ended, Euterpe smiled radiantly at Yobo. "This music will be the perfect beginning for my composition honoring human beings. It is the dawn of hope and beauty in a young world, is it not?"

Yobo stared at her. "I suppose—yes, it is."

"I would like to hear the full story," said Rembrandt.

"You tell the story, Admiral," said Jeff. "I wasn't conscious some of the time."

Yobo told the tale to Rembrandt and Euterpe, his rich voice rolling out the excitement, the danger, the humor (Jeff squirmed at the recounting of Mayla's interest in him), and the wild beauty of life on the paleolithic steppe of eastern Europe. "Jeff, I guess we'd better tell them about the other time track, but you'll have to do it because I wasn't there."

Jeff's story sent an odd stillness over the two Others sitting in the room. Euterpe looked down at her four hands and Rembrandt touched her shoulder lightly.

"I am glad I am not the Rembrandt you found in the false time track, someone who had no knowledge of you. Yet I believe that my sister would have liked to know that small human child, for she has not yet had children of her own."

"But I thank you for rescuing the child from that other Euterpe," she said tremulously, "because it meant that Boris Yobo would exist."

"Indeed," Yobo said with a gulp, "thank you, ma'am." He got to his feet and bowed to her. "I fear that we must go back to our own worlds."

"So soon?" Euterpe rose, this time as if it were she who was drawn up by hypnotic power. "You are welcome to visit the Others anytime. And I thank you for the music. Perhaps all music is not only a refuge from troubles, or an expression of feelings, but a symbolic way of describing reality itself, something none of us can understand completely."

"Beautiful." Yobo seemed to be breathing the word.

"But with the beauty of the things we create," Rembrandt said softly, "perhaps each of us contributes a piece of the understanding."

"Yes," said Yobo, taking Euterpe's right upper hand and putting it to his lips.

"Time to go," announced Norby.

"So soon?" Yobo said, echoing Euterpe.

90

She gazed up at him. "Perhaps each life is part of the music of reality that we all share. You and I."

"You and I," repeated Yobo.

"I think we'd better go *now!*" Norby shouted. "Remember that Jeff's long weekend is almost over and if we're late getting back to Space Academy he'll be in trouble."

"Good-bye, Euterpe. Until we meet another time," said Yobo.

Norby touched Jeff's arm. —Let's get him out of here, Jeff, before Space Command is minus its chief admiral again.

Jeff and Norby led Yobo back to his ship, where he sank into the control-room chair and sighed heavily.

"You know, Jeff, perhaps we shouldn't have told Euterpe about her other self wanting to keep the human child. She's rather fond of me, and for all we know these Others can juggle DNA around to make it possible for two completely different species to—"

"Why, Admiral!" Norby's head popped up to its fullest extent, his eyelids completely open. "Whatever is on your mind, sir?"

"Harrumph! Nothing. Nothing at all. Purely intellectual speculation. Take us directly to my home on Mars, Norby."

"But I have to go back on duty at the academy," said Jeff.

"We'll only spend a few minutes on Mars, cadet. I must return the family heirloom to my sister, and explain that I've had it, um, analyzed, and that it's from a woolly mammoth, not an African elephant."

"Maybe you'd better check to see that you still have the heirloom, Admiral," said Jeff, pointing to the safe.

"Great galaxy! What if we've changed history again and it isn't there!" said Yobo. "I'm almost afraid to open the safe. Are you sure you saw it in the hands of the chief when you were leaving the past?"

"Yes, sir. She tried to give it to me, but it wasn't finished the way you had it, sir. There wasn't anything carved on the bottom yet."

"Norby, you open the safe." Yobo clasped his hands together. "I'm just going to sit here and try to calm my nervous system. Rembrandt is right—time travel is dangerous."

"Here it is, Admiral," Norby said, the safe open.

Yobo turned the heirloom over and over. "The blasted thing seems exactly the same as it was when I put it in the safe. Don't you think so, Jeff?"

After looking it over, Jeff nodded. "The same, sir."

Norby chuckled metallically. "Humans are not very bright. The heirloom looks the same *because* we were part of history. Or rather because *I* was."

"What are you talking about!" Yobo roared.

"In the first place, I'm part of the history of that tusk because it was broken off when the mammoth hit my barrel."

"But Norby," Jeff said, "that was only in the history we created by going back in time. When the piece of tusk was carved the first time, in real history, the tribe may have taken it from the big bull mammoth after they killed it, or possibly scavenged its body."

"The bull was alive when we left," Yobo said, a puzzled frown on his face, "yet the tusk looks the same now."

"I tell you that I'm part of the history of that heirloom, and that I always was!" said Norby, pointing to it.

"Nonsense," said Yobo. "In real history, the bit of tusk was passed down through generations until it came to that cosmonaut great-great-granduncle of Wenoa's."

"Look at the bottom of the tusk," said Norby.

Jeff studied the tusk. The same half-moon shape and the mysterious dot were still there. Suddenly he gasped and turned the tusk, looking at the half-moon as he did so. When the curved part was uppermost, the dot was directly above the middle of the curve.

"You're right, Norby," Jeff said, beginning to laugh. "That's quite a time paradox, isn't it?"

"Cadet." Yobo spoke in an even deeper bass that sounded like the thunder heralding an awesome storm. "Explain!"

"It's simple, Admiral," said Norby. "After Jeff and I gave the little girl back to the tribe, the chief must have been so impressed by me that she carved my hat on the bottom of the ivory tusk."

"Impossible," said Yobo, squinting at the carving.

"It looks like it," said Jeff.

"Maybe," said Yobo. He put the heirloom into his tunic pocket. "I don't even want to think about the time paradoxes involved in this. Please don't ever tell my sister about it. If she wants to think it's a moon and star, let her. I think Muslims invaded Russia back when, so that will fit with her original theory about the carving. I mean, if I can manage to get her to accept that Wenoa is correct, and the heirloom is actually from the Grachev family."

"Good luck, Admiral," said Jeff.

"I'll need it."

14.

The Longest Weekend

Yobo opened the front door of his house and said, "The blasted butler isn't repaired yet!"

"If we'd stayed here for the weekend, instead of gallivanting through time and space, I could have fixed your robot butler."

"Norby," said Jeff, "the weekend was the way it was."

"Norby's right. We should have stayed here." Yobo walked into the hall and touched a wooden statuette from old Africa that was among the many objects on display.

"You'd never have met Euterpe," Jeff reminded him.

"Or seen her face shine when we played my ancestral music for her. My ancestors were many people, Jeff. And I like all of them."

"I'm glad, Admiral."

Yobo thumped Jeff on the back and led the way to the living room.

Two female faces looked up at them in surprise.

"What's the matter, Boris?" Eevee put down her teacup. "Why have you returned?"

"Perhaps he wanted to see me after all," said Wenoa, patting the couch next to her for Yobo to sit there. "Didn't you, Boro love?"

"Have you been here all weekend, Wenoa?"

"What are you talking about, Boris?" said Eevee. "You didn't answer my question. Why have you come back?"

"To return the heirloom, Eevee. Then we must hurry back to Space Command because I must work and Jeff must return to the academy."

"You never could make up your mind properly, Boris. First you insist on taking that holocamera with you on a trip, with a cadet and a robot to help you, and now you've decided to go back to work. Can't you ever take a decent vacation?"

"Vacation's over, Eevee."

Norby tugged at Yobo's uniform. "Admiral, sir . . ."

"Not now, Norby."

"But sir, I think I made a slight mistake. . . ."

"Norby—say, what day is this, Eevee?"

"Boris! Have you utterly lost your mind?"

Wenoa pulled Yobo down beside her. He looked dazed.

"Dear Boro, you and Jeff and Norby walked out of this room only an hour ago."

"I tried to tell you, sir," said Norby. "A slight miscalculation in ti—"

—Shut up, Norby [Jeff said telepathically, and added aloud, "we had to return because the admiral wants to see the documents you brought, the ones about the heirloom. Don't you, Admiral?"

"Oh, that's right." Yobo looked at Jeff gratefully. "Do show them to us, Wenoa."

Wenoa smiled. She was beautiful, too. "You see, darling Boro, that in the hour since you left, great changes have been wrought, changes that—"

"Changes? What changes?" Yobo scowled ferociously at Norby. "What have you done, you little metal monster!"

"Nothing, Admiral," squeaked Norby. "I was a little too efficient about the ti—I mean, our return. I didn't do anything else. I think."

"All of you are scatterbrained," said Eevee. "You certainly were as a child, Boris. It is astonishing that you grew up to become admiral. Sit down, Jeff. Have some more tea while Wenoa explains, if she can manage to do it without being too dramatic about it."

"I'm not sure I can stand hearing about changes," mut-

95

tered Yobo, "but I suppose I'd better find out what they are."

"Boro, love, our families are genuinely connected. I always felt the strong tie between us. . . ."

"Don't overdo it, Wenoa," Eevee said with her usual acerbity. "Where is the heirloom, Boris?"

Speechless, he handed it to her and stuffed a cookie into his mouth.

Jeff, hungry for any kind of ordinary Federation food, even afternoon tea, ate and hoped he didn't look too much like someone newly healed from being gored by a mammoth.

Wenoa put her hand on Yobo's thigh. "You must not get upset, dear. Even your dear sister did not mind too much when she realized the whole thing was legal."

"What whole thing?" Yobo croaked.

"Just let me show the heirloom to my children now and then. It will remain with you and Eevee, now that we know it genuinely belongs to your family."

"But it doesn't exactly. . . ." Yobo began.

"The heirloom belongs to both the Grachevs and the Yobos," said Eevee, making no motion to hand it to Wenoa. "But of course, now that there is proof that the Grachevs and the Yobos were once united. . . ."

Yobo sat back. "You accept that great-great-grandmother and that Russian cosmonaut—"

"Our parents taught us to revere the law, Boris. We must put up with the consequences of what our great-great-grandmother did."

"Ulp," said Yobo, taking a paper Wenoa had removed from the official-looking envelope she'd flourished in his face when he'd been trying to get away from her.

He read the paper and grinned. "Imagine that. A joint family tree, proving that my sister and I are partly descended from northern peoples. . . ."

"Roooosians!" Wenoa exhaled it. "Beautiful, wonderful

Russians, by way of the baby your great-great-grandmother had quite soon after the fateful Io mission. Not that I disparage the beautiful, wonderful people who contributed to the rest of my ancestry—why, I was even named after a beautiful, wonderful Native American. . . ."

"Wenoa, please show my brother the *other* paper."

When Yobo read the next paper, he laughed, and couldn't seem to stop. He handed the paper to Jeff, who smiled.

"Really, Boris," said Eevee. "I see nothing humorous about a marriage license. I suppose you'd have thought it more romantic if great-great-grandmother had *not* been legally married to her cosmonaut!"

"Oh, no, Eevee," said Yobo, still laughing. "I'm happy."

"This is only a copy of the license," said Wenoa. "Because the two cosmonauts married on board a spaceship, the captain officiating, the document was not properly registered at once. Then the ship had that accident on the Io mission and its computer records were mislaid. Mars was only a colony of the Federation at the time, and things were not straightened out for years. I have only recently been researching the archives, and with great difficulty I persuaded the stupid computers to disgorge the correct documents."

"I could have found them for you, ma'am," said Norby.

"You probably could have," said Wenoa. "You seem like a highly intelligent robot."

"Thank you, ma'am. If I were human, I'd vote for you."

At this moment, a small boy and girl ran into the room, holding hands.

"Can we have cookies, Grandma?" said Martin Luther Chen. "Natasha and I had a good time in the garden but we're hungry."

"Go ahead, dear," said Eevee. "Be sure to let Natasha have her share."

"Okay. I'm going to marry Natasha when I grow up." The two children took handfuls of cookies and ran out again.

"Don't faint, Eevee," said Wenoa, with a lovely smile. "Maybe they will, and it will be all right."

Elizabeth Victoria Yobo's nose was in the air, but she brought it down and said, "I have had many shocks in the last hour, Boris. I have accepted that our African heritage is not pure and that I am related to the Grachevs. Distantly, of course. Therefore you must accept—"

"But I do," said Yobo, patting Wenoa's thigh.

"I am referring," Eevee said frostily, "to the fact that I am not staying in the family mansion anymore. I am tired of being the caretaker of the Yobo antiques, including that elephant tusk given by great-great-grandmother to her legal husband. After his death, of course, it legally belonged to her again."

"Uh, it wasn't exactly like that. . . ." Yobo began.

"Please, Boris, don't interrupt. I am going to Federation Spome to be in Wenoa's new cabinet, as minister of culture."

"Congratulations, ma'am," said Jeff.

"Yes, congratulations, Eevee, and to you, Wenoa, for being part of our family." With careful gallantry, Yobo kissed Wenoa's hand, but when she bent toward him, he flung his arms around her, kissing her somewhat more thoroughly.

"Ah," Wenoa said, a little out of breath. "Then you'll spend the long weekend here, Boro?"

He sprang to his feet like a whale determined not to be beached in spite of the temptations. "Jeff, we must leave. Pictures. Lots of pictures. Right away. Come on, Norby. Good-bye, Eevee. Sorry, Wenoa. Until we meet again."

He strode from the room, Jeff and Norby running after him.

It seemed quiet and calm in the ship's control room until Yobo said, "Where's the holocamera?"

"You gave it to Norby, I think, at the same time you handed the child to him when you scared off the mammoth."

"Did I? I don't remember."

"I had it," said Norby.

"And?" asked Yobo.

"Please don't be angry, Admiral."

"Norby—what have you done?"

"I must have left it with the wrong Rembrandt, because I didn't have it after I took the child there. I'm sorry, sir."

"Then it's lost in time," said Yobo.

"I'll take my money out of savings and buy you a new one," Jeff said hurriedly, before Yobo could yell at Norby.

"No need, cadet. I have lost interest in cameras. And in family history. Perhaps someday I may explore the parts of Africa where the rest of my family originated—but then, the human family tree itself started in Africa."

"It's good to know that if you go back far enough, we're all related," said Jeff. "All humanity is one."

"Well put, cadet. If you ever need help searching out the branches of *your* family tree . . ."

"No, thank you, sir."

"Humans aren't everything," said Norby. "Didn't you enjoy Euterpe, Admiral?"

"Um. Women." Yobo gazed up at the ceiling of the *Pride.* "I think I will work at my desk in Space Command this entire weekend. Take us there, Norby. Do you mind going back, Jeff?"

"No, sir. I'll go on duty and the cadet who was taking my place can have a holiday. I don't think I'd like to live this long weekend again in any way but just quietly studying at the academy."

Norby took the ship into space, headed for the orbital wheel known as Space Command. They could see it glittering like a magic circle up ahead.

"Admiral," said Norby, "are you sure you don't mind being an admiral when on the other time track you were prime minister of the Federation?"

"What! That's a ridiculous question. . . ."

"I'm glad you're Admiral Yobo," said Jeff.

"Thanks. I want to stay admiral. I want to stay *me*—Boris Yobo, complete with my own memories, my own heritage, my own job, and . . . and . . ."

"Yes, Admiral?" said Jeff.

". . . and even with my own older sister."

"Really, Admiral?" asked Norby.

"Certainly, certainly. Older sisters aren't so bad. Especially when they are part of the family of an *admiral!* Prime Minister Yobo indeed! Bah!"